W

04

TERMINAL AVENUE

TERMINAL AVENUE

JIM CHRISTY

Ekstasis  Editions

National Library of Canada Cataloguing in Publication Data

Christy, Jim
    Terminal Avenue

    ISBN 1-894800-08-7

    I. Title.
    PS8555.H74T47 2002   C813'.54   C2002-910745-8
    PR9199.3.C4983T47 2002

Cover Art: Maurice Spira
Author Photo: Carol Ann Sokoloff

Acknowledgments: The author would like to thank the Woodcock
Fund for support during the writing of this novel.

Published in 2002 by:
Ekstasis Editions Canada Ltd.   Ekstasis Editions
Box 8474, Main Postal Outlet   Box 571
Victoria, B.C. V8W 3S1   Banff, Alberta ToL oCo

Terminal Avenue has been published with the assistance of a grant
from the Canada Council for the Arts and the Cultural Services
Branch of British Columbia.

*This book is for
Al MacLachlan*

CHAPTER ONE

Castle woke in the Rose Hotel when the blues came in the window. Slipped in with the weak sunlight under the dark green shade that was pulled to within an inch of the sill. The blues stated its case and a ship at the foot of Shanghai Alley added a baritone lament as if the behemoth was a brother sounding its camaraderie.

> *"Little girl, little girl…*
> *Where could you have gone"*

sang a clear, rich alto.

> *"Days have been so lonesome*
> *Nights have been too long."*

Louise Jones moaned as Castle swung his legs out of bed.

Yeah, pal. I know just how you feel, Castle mumbled. Don't let the fact that my companion here—I couldn't really call her a girl, especially not a little girl—don't let her presence lead you to jump to any conclusions. I mean just because we're curled up all cozy and warm on a lazy morning that doesn't mean we're like this every morning. No, sirree, Bill. You don't mind if I call you Bill? I get a feeling from the timbre of your voice that you are a Negro person, and I can't recall ever meeting or even hearing about any Negro person named Bob. Anyway, Bill, it is true that we've been together for about three weeks straight but for us, man, that's some kind of record. And Louise is about to take off on another tour to entertain the troops. Last month she came back just after the Nazis grabbed Norway. Woke up yesterday to find that Hitler and his boys waltzed into Paris. Paris! Makes a man afraid to go to sleep at night. We thought this thing would be over in a couple of months but it's been nearly a year now. Morale is down, so Louise is going to have to hit the road, show those boys her assets.

"What the hell you muttering about?"

"What a tender way to greet your guy. Why Louise, I was just telling Bill all about you, about your assets and…"

"Damn!"

Louise snatched at the sheet, pulled it up to her shoulders.

"Why didn't you tell me there was somebody…"

She looked about the room.

"What? Where…"

"Listen, here he is again."

The voice drifted up from the street:

> *"I been walking in round in circles*
> *Round and round and round*
> *Searching each and every*
> *Low down juke joint in town…"*

"Well the man has a soothing voice," Louise said, listening some more. "So nice that you feel sorry for him right away, him not having his little girl by his side. But at least he has you to talk to him. Wonder what he looks like."

Castle stood up, grabbed a towel, wrapped it around his middle, and walked over to the window. He pulled up the shade and looked down past the sign for the Rose Hotel, the rusted hulk of it, the neon tubing, and there on the other side of Cordova Street was a large Negro man sitting on a milk crate playing a guitar. He had a black patch over his left eye and he was wearing a white short sleeve shirt. The top of a harmonica peeked out of his shirt pocket. An upended fedora was between his feet.

The man finished the song, leaned back, scoped the street and licked his lips. Then he bent down and picked up the fedora, looked into it. Just seemed to stare at it, like if he stared long enough, more coins would appear—coins or ration stamps, even. Anything.

"Well?" said Louise.

"Well he looks like a fellow what's had the blues."

"I wonder where his little girl got to."

"She done left him, rode the plush back to San Francisco."

"Well this not-so-little girl of yours is going to have to ride the plush soon enough, so why don't you get back here and remind her of what she'll be missing."

Castle turned from the window and smiled as he took in the sight of Louise Jones stretched across the bed.

"Why, Gene Castle. What ever could you be hiding under that towel?"

He had gotten two steps closer to the bed when the old Russian alarm clock sounded. He thought of it as Russian because it was shaped like a cobblestone a young hot head in St. Petersburg might have picked up and thrown at a cossack during the Revolution. And it always went off like *The Rites of Spring.*

"Damn! When are you going to get rid of that goddamned thing? As many times as I've heard it, it still shocks the bejesus out of me."

Castle hammered the clock into submission and climbed into bed. He grabbed an end of the sheet and started unwinding. "I like the wrapping," he said. "Now let's see about the present."

9

Fifteen minutes later, Gene and Louise were leaning back against the headboard. Louise had the sheet pulled up to her breasts and seemed to be studying her chest which was flushed red.

She reached for the empty glass next to the alarm clock on the bedside table, and pressed it against her chest. Then she lifted the glass and looked at the pale circle in the blush.

"Looks," Castle said, "like you fell asleep in the sun with your rye and water balanced on your chest."

"Funny, I can have two in a row but the flush never gets deeper. Wonder why that is?"

"Beats me. I can't figure out why you flush red in the first place."

"You must have come across the phenomenon somewhere during your vast experience of women and the world?"

"A few times, it is true but…"

Louise reached behind her for the pillow and whacked him with it on the side of the head.

"Just kidding."

"Yeah, sure."

"Seriously, Louise. It is a marvel, your chest. The firm swelling of the breasts there above the top of the sheet."

"You mean they're not firm below the top of the sheet?"

"Of course that's not what I mean. They're an anatomical marvel those breasts."

"Are they like ripe melons, the way they write it in those books they keep behind store counters and only offer to you if you come in with a sneaky expression and wearing a long overcoat?"

"No, they're like melons that aren't ripe yet. Yours are firmer than ripe melons."

"They're not as good as my legs but they're all right. I like them but I'm not going to get carried away with it. Reminds me of that dame with Wonder Shows back in '31."

"Who's that?"

"Kooch girl. Called herself Trixie Nicks. This was after you went off with Billy Buttons to run the Ten-in-One. She was from some place like Manyberries, Saskatchewan, though by the airs she put on, you'd think she was straight from the boulevards of Paris. Yeah, rue Blondel. All right, I hate to admit it but she was a good-looking piece; had a fine form but an exaggerated appreciation of what she had been blessed with, as if it was all her own doing. She was only five foot four but she had a way of looking down her nose at people who were taller than her."

"She liked women?"

"No. If she'd have considered them, it would have been the same thing, none of them good enough for her. Yet, at nighttime there were some weird sounds coming from her trailer which was next to mine. I mean, some wailing and moaning and Russian alarm clock noises. Louder than that tattooed bitch you used to hang out with…"

"Okay. Let's skip the part where you pretend not to remember her name."

"I sincerely don't remember her name, only that she couldn't have been any spring chicken. Hell, those ugly tattoos of hers had faded back in '24."

"Okay, back to the other one."

"Trixie Nicks. It was herself she loved. That frail fancied her own tail, you might say. And every night she took advantage."

"She hang a red scarf over the lampshade, put on her satin teddy, play a little Lester Young on the Victrola, slip between the satin sheets and whisper in her own ear, as it were?"

"Maybe, but sometimes I think she just pounced on herself like she was Jean Harlow and a bush ape been in the woods six months, both at the same time."

"Ain't it something, Louise, the characters one meets?"

"Fucking A, Gene."

"Well then accompany your almost ripe breasts, your Barabara Stanwyck legs and your incomparable rear end into the washroom and get ready so we can hit the streets and meet more of them."

Half an hour later, Gene and Louise walked through the familiar black-and-white-tiled vestibule of the Rose Hotel and out on to Cordova Street, all abustle with citizens headed toward actual jobs. The Negro man across the way was serenading them, and their lunch buckets tapped their legs in time.

"Look at them marching along with womanly purpose," commented Louise. "I'm so proud to see those sisters of mine wearing slacks like Marlene Dietrich, head rags like Aunt Jemima, going to catch the ferry for to carry them to rivet-catching jobs in North Van shipyards. And our youth—youths? Why, just a year ago they were wasting their lives in Relief Camps, now their rushing off to save democracy."

"Yeah, and the Army's paying a dollar-thirty a day compared to the Camps' twenty cents. Not that that has anything to do with it. But it is a beautiful day so I won't spoil it by thinking anymore about the state of the world—at least not for a couple of minutes because to get to work I have to pass Woody's newsstand. Anyway, just ahead as we approach Main Street, I spy another fellow who's rushing this way. See him?"

"That must be Henry 'the Hipster' Heinz."

They were referring to a tall and very thin party in a tight-fitting black suit, the cuffs of which ended several inches above the tops of black and white wingtips revealing ankles that bulged like a pair of adam's apples in skinny legs. The man had a pencil-line moustache and his conk was topped by a toupee that appeared to have been treated with KY Jelly. He was swinging his arms and mumbling to himself as he stepped onto the curb and almost bumped into them.

"Huh? Oh! Well, diggity-diggity-do. It is Gene Castle and his not-so-frail, the aw-reet and not-so-petite, Louise."

"Good to see you too, Henry," Louise said. "But enough with the size references."

"Solid."

"You're right about that," Louise said.

"Where you off to with such determination and hustle so

early in the morning?" Gene asked. The thin man transferred his weight from one foot to the other and back again, nodded his head, pulled at his long nose, tugged at a fleshy ear lobe, muttered, "Hmm, ah hmm. Yes, Gene, well, you see, it seems or, at least, what I'm told, is that last night or maybe it was early this morning, I was coming from the Three Deuces and I fell out on the street. I find that hard to believe, of course."

Louise frowned and shook her head. "That's not like you, Henry."

"Hell, it ain't. Or, Hell it wasn't. I mean, I've changed. Don't mess with the pipe or them ungodly goofballs." He sniffed. "Anyway, somebody copped my axe, my horn, my precious C-Melody saxophone what's been with me since Dixieland was king. Not that I ever played that shit."

"Thank God for that."

"Gene, aw-reet. Now, the word come up from the lower forty-eight that there's some new music happening. It'll take awhile to cross the line, but it'll get here in time. Yes, yes. Call it rebop. Sounds like a Chinese orchestra on goofballs. But, me, you dig, Lester's my man. If you don't play like Lester, you're wrong, Jack."

"If I could play," Gene said, "I'd play like Lester."

"Diggity-diggity-do to that, gates. Prez in back of Lady Day on 'Yesterdays' or anything."

"I'm with you, Hipster."

"Solid, daddy-o. Now I got to cut out, find my Melody, visit my man, if you know what I'm laying down."

"Aw-reet," Louise said.

The man took a step like a racehorse breaking from the gate, stopped suddenly, spun on the heels of his black-and-whites, said, "Hey, dig it. If I don't have any luck-arouti maybe I'll hire you to find my ever-loving axe."

"Solid."

"Later."

Henry broke into his litany of nods to interject a more

enthusiastic one and kept walking, the way Gene and Louise had come, down Cordova Street whistling a tune.

"Look at him go," said Gene. "Whistling 'Tickle-toe.'"

"That there is a man for whom a world war is of no significance."

"Wonder how the lanky son-of-a-gun would pay me if I did find his horn."

"No doubt with bennies."

Main Street on a warm, sunny morning in the latter part of June. Castle pictured all the Main Streets of Canada, all a bustle, merchants rolling down their awnings, greeting the folks and the brand new business day. Everybody with smiles on their lips and a top o' the morning to you. Sure there was a war on and thousands were being killed and worse but you couldn't carry the burdens of the world on your shoulders and, anyway, our boys hadn't seen action yet, at least not with any Germans. The ones overseas were at bases in England, busting out now and again to hit the pubs and form attachments with the flowers of English maidenhood, and no doubt having to duke it out with the locals on account of it.

But there was one fellow on the corner up ahead who wasn't smiling. Manny Israel. He never really smiled, come to think of it, but faced the world with a permanent look of bemusement from the doorway of his store. For a couple of decades, he'd sold used items, castoffs, beneath a hand-painted sign that announced: Manny's Junk. But then war was declared, the Depression ended, and Manny, who had no flies on him, got a new *modus operandi*, not to mention a professional sign, painted by a goyishe but nevertheless reliable friend of his brother-in-law's. So for a year and a half, he had presided over the ever-so-successful Manny's New Stuff.

"So, Louise. Gene. Good morning to you. If I am not remiss calling it a good morning what with what is happening in the world."

They greeted the big man with the big belly and unusual copper-coloured hair. Manny used to have a thick full head of it but over the last few years was losing it rapidly and between wisps you could see scalp which was the exact colour of chicken skin.

Manny glanced up and down the street, and gestured for Gene and Louise to come closer toward him. When they did, Manny said, "So, Gene. Before you ask me out of politeness how business is, let me tell you that it is good and so good that I can afford to put some aside."

"That's wonderful, Manny."

"Thank you. Now, ask yourself, how often is it, you ask a guy how business is, he tells you it's good?"

"Not bloody often," said Louise.

"All right, so I tell you this, what does it mean?"

"Anybody else, a business type, asking me that," Castle said, "I'd figure he was leading up to asking me for a loan and wants his business to seem like a thriving concern worth investing in, but this can't be the situation here because you know me well enough to know I'm a happy-go-lucky so-and-so who lives for today and never saves a dime."

"Exactly."

"So what gives?"

"All joking aside, Gene. Here's the thing. I'm making the moo-la and so are most of my friends, some of whom you've met in the backroom of the store as I'm sure you remember from a year ago—can it only be one year?—when we had a meeting to figure out what to do about that Sherman Redman character."

"I remember. I miss the guy from that meeting who got dead."

"Poor Larry Sobell. So, anyway, you may recall also there was Danny Klein. Who would believe that Danny Klein, a guy who spent a lot of those days feeling sorry for himself—and who could blame him really, him losing his legs in Spain which you know all about—who'd believe he'd stop feeling sorry for him-

15

self and started getting rich?"

"Well, I guess if you say so, it must be true."

"Uh huh. Well, while you were off hiding or whatever it was you were doing just after we got in the war, Danny got a job—is this what they mean by irony?—with the Goodasnew Prosthetic Limb company, corner of Princess and Gore, where you killed that Nazi."

"Irony, chance and their flamboyant and sometimes too conspicuous younger brother, coincidence, rule the world, I do believe."

"Yeah, well, he became an advisor and liason with amputees and people born without limbs and they developed methods that put them at the head of the industry and all that which I won't get into except to say that Danny-boy is rich."

"Excuse me, Manny but I have to go to rehearsal."

"Just a minute, Louise, if you can spare it. Here's the thing. We figure, Gene, you're the man."

"For what?"

"Go kill Hitler."

"Oh, well, I'm busy today, Manny. Can I get to it next week?"

"I'm serious. Listen, hire whoever you need to help. Round up a crack team of compatriots. Maybe that Leandro Martine fellow I heard so much about. We'll pay whatever it costs. Pay gladly."

"You're not thinking like a businessman, Manny."

"Why do you say that?"

"Somebody bumps off Adolf and it's back to Manny's Junk. Back to the Depression. And me…"

"You'd be a hero."

"I'd be a villain. The guy who returned the youth of the free world to the bread lines."

"Well, think about it."

"I promise."

They went west on Hastings, hoofed it a few blocks and up ahead noticed a commotion near the intersection with Carrall Street, which was their destination.

"I see three harness bulls and Koronicki's car," said Castle.

"It would be nice, a law-abiding couple such as we are, if we could go out of a morning for breakfast without reminders of life's seamier aspects."

"Is that from one of your scripts?"

"No, we try to keep things light-hearted, keep our boys minds off the negative and on the finer things. Like my rear end."

"And the rest of it."

When they got closer, half a block away, they could hear the foghorn voice of Chief of Detectives, Horace Koronicki giving orders to the trio of harness bulls. "MacLachlan get statements from the witnesses. Olafson, Murphy keep the crowd back."

Koronicki turned his attention to another guy in a suit, his young assistant, Detective Danny Bartoli, a good-looking man more than six feet tall with a long but elegant Roman nose. The detectives were standing, one on either side, of a body that was face down on the pavement.

Koronicki spied Gene and Louise, pointed a stubby thumb at the dead man, said, "Buys it right out front of the Only Seafood Restaurant. Think he was disappointed it wasn't open yet? Maybe they could take a photograph, blow it up, put it in the window. Nice little caption, 'They're just dying to get in the Only.' What d'you think, Castle?"

Louise answered for him, "I think maybe you've been on the job too long."

"Well you're right about that."

Detective Bartoli, who was the nephew of a bad guy Castle had beaten up years ago, said, "Like your suit, Gene, but it's grounds for arrest."

"Yeah," said his boss. "You should know better than to wear a double-breasted which have been outlawed since this war began. We'll have to take you in."

"That law only applies to new suits bought after we weren't smart enough to listen to J. S. Woodsworth."

"Whaa?" asked Koronicki.

"Let me translate," said Louise. "He means since Canada declared war."

"Yeah," Castle said. "And I haven't been able to afford a new suit since we stopped driving on the left."

"When was that?" the Chief asked. "Twenty-one, twenty-two?"

"I'm not sure," Castle said, "Sounds like a question for that guy on the radio."

"You mean Mister Smartypants?" asked Bartoli.

"He's the one."

"Only a kike could be that smart," Bartoli said.

"You mean there's no chance he's a wop?"

Bartoli fixed Castle with a hard stare. Castle smiled at him but held the stare.

"Oh, which reminds me," Louise said, breaking it up. "I'm going to be a guest on his show later this week."

"Why, Louise," Bartoli said, looking at her as if she was the most fascinating thing he'd ever seen. "That's wonderful…"

"You can call her Louise after business hours," Koronicki said. "She's Miss Jones while you're working."

Bartoli smirked.

"Hey, Horace, he called me Gene, and you didn't say anything."

"Horace?" said Bartoli.

"I hate to interrupt your pleasant badinage—remember that word, Koronicki?" Castle interrupted. "But you remind me of neighbours in lovely Marpole or someplace, chatting over a fence. One neighbour obviously with a crush on another one, trying to flirt with her while the nosey neighbourhood curmudgeon observes it all. Only thing is, instead of a fence, you got a dead man."

Koronicki and Bartoli looked down at the body as if surprised it hadn't gotten up and trundled off.

"A bindle stiff by the look of him. Wandered a little too far from the train yards. Got shanked. Turn him over, Danny."

The tall detective bent and grasped the corpse's shoulders. Castle noticed Bartoli's wide wrists and big hands. He wasn't a heavy man but raw-boned.

The body had been lying on a pillowcase that was soaked with blood and stuffed with clothes. Castle recognized the man from the old days but hoped it wouldn't show, aware that Koronicki was watching him, always watched him whenever a dead person was in the area.

"So, Gene. I mean Castle. A bindle buddy of yours?"

"What makes you think he'd be a buddy of mine?"

"Look on your face. You were quick to cover up but not quick enough."

Castle was about to tell the Chief that he didn't recognize the deceased. It was an automatic reaction and a good one: never tell a cop the truth. Unless the cop was something like a friend, especially one you might need when you were in Castle's line of work. He was a private eye of sorts. The sort you came to when there was no one else. To some jokers, Castle was known as The Last Resort.

"Professor Treherne. He was a good man. An old Wobbly. Had been riding the rails since the Eighties."

"What was his real name?"

"Don't know. Don't know anyone who might know. He was always known as Professor."

"What was he a professor of?"

"Roadology."

"Just an old radical," Koronicki said, dismissively.

"A bolshevik," Bartoli said, contempt in his voice.

"No, Bartoli. He was no bolshevik. And, Koronicki, you can say he was just an old radical but it was guys like him who got little children like your grandson out of the coal mines. The

Professor was best known as a workingman's songwriter. I'm sure you and your buddies sit around the stationhouse, singing some of his tunes, like 'Riot in Winnipeg' and 'When I Meet All the Strawbosses in Hell.'"

"Yeah, sure thing," Koronicki grunted.

"I know one of his you have probably heard of."

"Don't play with me no more, Gene. I mean, Castle."

"'Girl of the Orchards.'"

"Yeah, I heard of that one."

"It is a beautiful song," Louise said. "My daddy used to sing it:

> *I met her in the Okanagan*
> *When cherries were ripe on the vine*
> *I knew from the moment I saw her*
> *That this girl had to be mine.*"

Louise turned away with tears in her eyes, started walking.

Castle gave the Professor another look, said to Koronicki, "Find out who did it, Horace."

"Don't call me…" He was going to add "that in *public*" but didn't say it. Instead, turned to his partner, shook his head, "Danny, you think, an old flatfoot gets it *in public*, people going to be broken up about it?"

CHAPTER TWO

Louise had turned the corner at Carrall by the time Gene caught up to her, and they made for the steamy windows of Ramona's Deluxe Café, just off the alley near the corner of Pender. The windows were always like that, too steamy to see inside, though somebody like Gene Castle or somebody like Louise Jones could count on knowing who would be on the other side of the glass. It was, therefore, no surprise to push open the door and see the usual characters. Nor was it a surprise to almost trip over a suitcase at the threshold, because there was always someone in Ramona's who'd just gotten off a liner or was just about to board, who'd ridden a sidedoor pullman over the mountains, or even motored north from the U. S. of A. Quite often these individuals were on the lam and they were safe in Ramona's as long as they passed the test. The test was not written down anywhere. There were no rules of comportment. If you watched your manners, didn't upset the feeling of the place, never hawked religious tracts and didn't rat out anyone you knew to be hiding in the basement earning his or her keep by peeling potatoes, then you could stay.

Matty Muldoon, the old man with the lobster red face and

eyelids like walnuts, slits for eyes, bags underneath them big enough to pack caulk boots, wearing stagged britches and two full sets of longjohns—he'd passed the test, passed it long, long ago, back in the Earlies when Ramona owned the place. He was the only one who knew who Ramona was and Matty wasn't telling, despite numerous attempts over the decades to get it out of him. Why, little Joe Frontenac in the last booth, ace reporter and author of the wildly popular 'I Was There' column in the *Times* had been wheedling, cajoling, begging and offering Matty real money for the answer nearly every single day since Castle had introduced the two of them, a few years earlier.

Matty moved his hands and you saw there had had been a mug of tea between them. He touched a finger to his cap when he noticed Gene and Louise, and continued telling a story from his days at sea to a young fellow on the next stool. Fellow had 'drifter' written all over him. You had to wonder these days how a lad that age stayed out of the service.

Guy Roberts, the king of sugar, was at his usual place along the counter and, as usual, Raymond Thomas was by his side. Raymond pretended to be Guy's chauffeur, even wore a little admiral's cap sometimes, one given him by Gene Castle after an adventure a year or so earlier but, in reality, Mr. Thomas was Mr. Roberts' partner and financial adviser. The masquerade was necessary because Thomas was a Negro person and Roberts was not.

There were a few others in there that they recognized. As they settled into the booth with Joe Frontenac, Louise said, "That working girl at the end of the counter is giving you the look."

Castle glanced at the dame. Everything about her said she was twenty-five; everything but the eyes. The dame looked at Castle, at Louise and looked away.

Castle shrugged. "She looks kind of familiar."

"Is there anything you want to tell me, Gene?"

"There's a lot I want to tell you Louise but I'd prefer to whisper it in your ear when we're all alone, and Joe isn't listening."

"What's that?" Frontenac asked.

"Nothing, Joe," Louise said. "Just some scuttlebutt that would probably make a good story for you but mum's the word."

Maude stopped at the table to unburden herself of two of the eight cups of coffee she carried in her hands. "Usual?"

"Just the coffee for me," Louise said.

"Let me have some flapjacks," said Castle.

Maude turned away, shouted, "Stack a'three" to the antique owner and grill man, Tommy Chew, whose head and shoulders were occasionally to be seen in the window-opening between restaurant and kitchen. Old Tommy's upper body bobbed and weaved, his arms fluttered like he was conducting a miniature orchestra on his grill. In the background, hanging on hooks on the kitchen wall, were copper-bottomed pots that reminded Castle of the back of Manny Israel's head.

When miffed at a customer, Tommy shouted in Cantonese. He sometimes spoke seriously in Cantonese to Maude who understood no Cantonese. Tommy's other attempts at communication consisted of brusque gestures and grill man's English. No matter how many years you'd been falling by Ramona's Deluxe Café, it was still disconcerting to hear Tommy cry, "Order up! Two on a raft with oars."

"You can joke away my friends," said the handsome reporter. "But deadline fast approaches and I'm drier than Osoyoos in August."

Louise shook her head, feigning sympathy, "That's real dry, pardner."

"Yeah, make fun if you want but you don't know what real pressure is."

Gene made steeple of his eyebrows.

"Okay, maybe you do. But this kind of pressure is different. I'm desperate enough, I may have to go out to the Kitsilano Pavilion tomorrow and scope out the Women's Weightlifting Championship. Thing's sponsored by *Health and Physique* magazine which, it turns out, has a page devoted to women weightlifters."

"You are kidding?" Louise said.

"Am not, alas. I hear they have some tough characters that'll be there."

"You are desperate, Little Joe."

"Yeah. Too bad I never got to meet that fellow who was in here last year. Just saw him the one time. Remember? Guy you knew or knew of. We were having a drink, celebrating Raymond getting out of the hospital."

"Guy looked," Louise said, "like he should have been the vamp's boyfriend?"

"Yeah, Galatea Monti."

"Get the moon look off your face, Joe," said Louise. "It is not becoming."

"Can't help it, that dame. Anyway, yeah, that was the guy. Martine something."

"Leandro Martine," said Castle.

"I got a feeling he would have made a good story. You heard from him, Gene?"

"No, he's one of those here-today-gone-tomorrow kind of guys. Look for him in Vancouver and he turns up in Valparaiso."

"Oh, well. Maybe some day. In the meantime, well, I'm a guy who's used to prowling the streets for his stories, see? Dropping into cafés and bars and afterhours' joints. Seeing society high and low, taking the pulse of it, and sketching it for my readers most of whom have nary a notion of these goings on. I'm the guy with his collar turned up, fedora pulled down over his eyes trudging through the rain, hands in the pockets of his trenchcoat, notebook in there, scribbling as I go."

"So that's what you do," Louise said, "when you have your hands in your pockets like that. Why, I thought…"

"Jest, if you must…"

"Jest?" repeated Castle. "What the hell's wrong with you today?"

"You interrupted me. Where was I?"

"You were walking in the rain," Louise said, "pretending to be working."

"Oh, yeah. I'm the guy smoking a cigarette at the counter, lamping the joint over, I'm the guy scoping the shipyard, hanging out at Army-Navy…"

"Looking for girls," said Louise.

"Well that too. What I am is the guy who Was There. I'm the Restif de la Bretonne of this burg. So to be without a story is particularly humiliating."

"Who?" said Louise.

"I heard he was a fink," Castle said.

"You've heard of Restif?"

"You needn't be so surprised. I was in the hoosegow down in Panama one time with some sort of knockabout semi-criminal, sailor-type who knew all about the bird. This gent's name was Maq-something. You know, one of those guys speaks a dozen languages but you can't figure his nationality. Anyway, he said it broke his heart when he found out Restif was in the pay of the cops."

"It just about broke my heart," Frontenac said.

"Yeah, well, look Joe. I'll give you a story. Hate to do it. I mean, I hate that it happened. You ought to finish up your java and dash around the corner where your story's lying dead on the pavement. Guy named Professor Treherne."

"Guy that wrote 'Girl of the Orchards'?"

"Yeah."

"I'm on my way."

Frontenac stood, took coins from his pocket, dropped them on the table, patted himself down, bid them a hasty, "See you," and got out of there. Castle watched him scurry away. It was even more disconcerting to see Joe Frontenac stand up than it was to hear Tommy Chew speak grill man's English, the reason being that the reporter was devilishly handsome—you could imagine his face on the movie poster about the swashbuckling pirate who roamed the seven seas getting into sword fights and having bodices ripped on his behalf in every port—but he was, and this was the bane of his existence, only five-foot-five. Castle had seen it so many times, in Vancouver, in Spain, in France, usually in a tavern or saloon, some good-looking dame giving Frontenac the eye, and Frontenac, sitting there, giving it back, knowing what was coming, knowing that sooner or later he would have to stand up.

So Joe left Ramona's, then they watched Clarence Thomas and Guy Roberts leave, Clarence limping with his cane. Louise saying, "You know, Gene. One thing about Clarence always bothered me was that he always seemed haughty, stand-offish or something. I mean, a tall, handsome well-dressed fellow like that but he didn't give off anything."

"Yeah, Laura Easely, said the same thing about him once."

"Hmmph! I'm sure there's not much about men that one doesn't know."

"As you were saying about Clarence?"

"That bitch has always fancied you."

"I only have eyes for you."

"Has she ever…"

"Do I say anything about your legions of admirers?"

"Yeah, okay. All right. So Clarence with that cane. It somehow humanizes him."

"Hell of a way to get humanized. Get run over by a Packard a couple of times."

Louise looked up at the big clock on the wall—it was on one side of a glass-doored pie cabinet that had never, as far as Castle knew, ever contained a pie. On the other side of the cabinet was a framed, hand-coloured and enlarged photograph of a Chinese man wearing a green suit jacket, blue shirt and green tie. Most people assumed it was an earlier Mr. Chew; Castle wondered if it might not be Ramona's husband.

"Well, I've got to make rehearsal."

"Okay, sweetheart. Say, are you really going to be on the

Mister Smartypants show?"

"Sure thing. This war's good for us entertainers."

They kissed each other goodbye, then Louise took a couple of steps, looked over her right shoulder at the back of her right leg.

"Are my seams straight?"

"Let me take a second, follow the seams all the way up."

"You'll get a chance to do that soon enough, you play your cards right."

Five minutes later, Castle left Ramona's carrying two cardboard cups of coffee. He walked to the corner of Pender Street where the little man with the hunched back was hawking papers, talking in headlines:

"Nazis Stroll Into Paris…Roads Clogged as Thousands Flee City of Light…Getchernews here!"

"How about a paper, bud?"

"Hey, Gene. Here you go, buddy."

"Whaddya know, Woody? Whaddya say?"

"I know tragedy sells papers and my hump still hurts. Might be worse, I could be a hunchback in times when nothing was happening."

"You remember times like that?"

"Not since I was what they call in the movies a 'papoose.'"

"I'd like to stay and hear again about how your family crossed the plains braving attacks from other Indian braves and you lying there on the travois, but I got to go on account of the coffee's getting cold and Laura'll throw a snit fit."

"Yeah, Gene. I wish some dame'd throw a snit fit over something I done, or I didn't…do. I almost said 'didn't done.'"

"You did."

"Did what?"

"You did done it."

"Huh?"

"Said 'did done it.'"

"Have it your way, Gene. And, by the way, Louis-Godoy is less than a week from now."

"Thanks, I'll go see Beanie Brown."

Castle crossed the street to the Standard Building. Holding a coffee container in each hand, he nudged the revolving door with the toe of his shoe and watched a tableau of the street shatter and reform itself. He caught a glimpse of the corner of Shanghai Alley and the characters drawn on a sign that looked real exotic but he knew meant: Rooms to Let.

Laura Easely was sitting at the far end of the marble floored lobby in her little alcove, on the other side of a dutch-door working at her new switchboard. She looked up, a wire in each hand, "Good morning, sweetheart. I mean, Gene."

"Gorgeous. Here's your coffee. You know, I figure I've been bringing you coffee for five years now and, therefore, you must owe me a heap of dough."

"No, way. Five years sounds impressive but you've been away for four years and two months of it."

"I guess you're right. How's it coming with the new machine?"

"I'm still slow. I liked the old one better. Guess I'm just an old-fashioned girl. I'm just like you in a way."

"What do you mean? You think I'm an old-fashioned girl too?"

"No, silly. You and me. Plugging and unplugging. That's what we do, only not with each other."

"I thought you weren't going to talk about that kind of thing."

"I'm not."

"Good. I see you've been to the beauty parlour."

"Girl's got to take care of herself even more these days. Less men around."

Laura was wearing a tailored brown suit, open-necked, starched white blouse under it so you could just see the top of the 'v' of her breasts, her chest dusted with freckles, strands of a gold chain coming together and disappearing.

"You're doing a good job of it."

"What?"

"Taking care of yourself."

She looked in his eyes, looked away. Sipped her coffee.

"Oh, yeah. I almost forgot. You have a visitor."

"Thanks for finally telling me. Is he upstairs?"

"She. She's upstairs."

"Is she...?"

"No, she's no bombshell. Nor rounder neither. More the middle-aged-housewife-type. You ever had one of those?"

"In my office?"

"Any place?"

"No. So I'd best be going."

"Okay. You got a message too."

"I'm sure you've read it, so what does it say?"

"Says, 'An old acquaintance would like to see you.'"

Laura handed him an envelope his name on the outside, the sentence written on plain paper.

"Written in a man's hand. What did he look like?"

"Didn't see him. It was slipped under my door when I got in this morning."

"Is Renny in? Maybe he saw the guy."

"I already asked and he said he hadn't."

"Okay, thanks."

"Poor kid," Laura said.

"Who, Renny?"

"Yeah. I went looking for him, heard him talking. Thought he was auditioning to do the fights on radio."

"What'd you mean?"

"He was in his janitor's closest, door half open. I hear, 'Here's the bell for the second round. Falcone moves cautiously toward the centre of the ring. Weeks rushes to meet him, feints with the left, throws a right hand lead over the gloves of Falcone and down he goes.' Like that."

"Did he get up?"

"Falcone? Yeah, then Renny knocked him down three more times and they stopped the fight."

"You think Ronny'll call his last fight?"

"The Mendoza fight? Ronny's punchy but I don't think he's crazy."

"I better go."

Castle liked the lady right away. He climbed the two flights of stairs, turned left and there she was down at the end of the hall, standing patiently between his door, which had

GENE CASTLE
9 - ?

painted in black letters on frosted glass, and that of bookie Beanie Brown's which had nothing painted on it.

When he approached, and flashed what he hoped was his most engaging smile, the woman smiled back albeit tentatively. She didn't regard him with the expression of a dyed in the wool scold, nor did she look at her watch and go, "Tssk, tssk," even though it was ten minutes past nine.

No, the woman—she was probably in her late-forties—in her best woman's home auxiliary outfit, conservative shoes, hat and gloves, said, "Mr. Castle?"

"Yes, ma'am."

She looked so humble, Castle found himself apologizing for being late. The lady nodded as if she understood all about how one was so easily detained in these trying times. Then she said that she'd never done this kind of thing before.

The way she said it, the tremulous quality to her voice, Castle had a thought of the two of them glancing left and right before getting down on the marble floor to couple right there in the hallway. I've never done this kind of thing before.

"Well, let me open up and we'll go inside and you can tell me whatever you want to tell me."

He unlocked his door, held it open for the woman, prepared himself for her expression of shock at seeing his furnishings. Laura once advised him to talk to prospective customers in the hallway, get their signature on the contract before bringing them inside.

Castle liked his office. If you were supposed to get a sense of a person from the person's surroundings his office did the job. Yeah, and some might say that was precisely the problem.

Seven feet from the door was a lacquered Chinese screen that served to partition off what one day he might get up the nerve to call 'the waiting room.' Not that the two chairs had ever been occupied while he was on the other side of the screen talking to a client. Not that one of them had ever been occupied.

So you stepped around the screen and looked across the big room at two tall, double-hung windows and under the windows was a radiator thick with gray paint. Over the radiator a sturdy cedar shelf held half a set of the Coronation Edition of the *Encyclopedia Britannica*, flanked by a bottle of rum and a bottle of rye. Castle worked, when he worked, at an oak desk that was six feet long and while sitting in a captain's chair also made from oak. He had a new radio in a brown case with big knobs and it took up the right far corner of his desk. Two ladderback chairs faced the desk.

But what is between the screen and the desk, Castle thought, ah, that is what makes the room the masterpiece it is. There was the beautiful rug that Castle had swiped from an office above a whorehouse owned by a gangster who wouldn't be needing it for sixty years, which was when he'd be getting out of the prison. Castle calculated he had about fifty-six years left before having to return the rug. Augie Garmano'll be near on one hundred and twenty years old by then. I wonder what he'll look like, Castle mused to himself.

He noticed the woman looking at the rug. It really was special. Nine by twelve, it showed a map of Italy in pale yellow, outlined in red against a background of middle blue.

"Please have a seat," he told the woman, fearful that she might notice the photographs on the wall of men with rifles and others in satin shorts with their hands in boxing gloves, and decide to run away. If that didn't to it there were the four masks, Haida, Dahomey, Mosquito and Balinese.

She kept to the perimeters of the carpet and sat primly on one of the chairs facing the desk, folded her hands on her lap and crossed her feet at the ankles like she was having her picture taken with the rest of the women at the bake sale to raise money for our boys Over There, as they used to call it in the last big war.

Castle hung his fedora on, rather than sailed it toward, a hook on his driftwood hat rack. He sat in his sturdy captain's chair, vowed to eschew his usual sarcasm unless, dammit, the woman left him no recourse, and cleared his throat. When that elicited no response, he asked her how he might be of service.

"It's my son, Billy."

She didn't so much say it, as pronounce it and with finality so Castle had the feeling he should understand the situation at once. As if everyone knew darling Billy and what he was forever getting up to. Castle was put in mind of a situation in Dawson City, Yukon. He was up there for a while in the late-twenties, lying low after some escapades with Sandina down Nicaragua way. There was a young fellow, used to come into the Bank of Commerce every month and rob the place. Same bank where Robert Service had worked. So, this fellow, who was named Tommy, not Billy, would flee the bank with the canvas sacks of money and head back home. Twenty-six years old and still lived at home, in the family cabin with Ma and Pa. Later, the day of the robbery or the next day if they were busy, the Mounties would come around to the cabin. Ma or Pa would open the door, see the Mounties. One of the Mounties would nod his head and Ma or Pa would nod back, say, "We'll get the boy."

"What did Billy do, ma'am? He rob the bank again?"

"Why lordy. What an unusual thing to ask. My Billy is a good boy."

"I apologize. For a moment, I had him confused with someone else."

"You think you know my Billy?"

"No, not at all. But why don't you tell me all about him and what's bothering you. You might start by letting me know his last name and your last name."

"Myerhoff. Billy Myerhoff. And I'm Nora Myerhoff."

Castle was surprised. He would have figured her to be a Gladys or Hilda. Or, perhaps 'Anne,' after the parton saint of housewives. 'Noreen' seemed too racy a handle for the respectable party facing him. Maybe she was racy in her day. No, he doubted that.

"As you know, I'm Gene Castle."

"Yes. Now, my son."

"Billy."

"Yes. Billy, he's only eighteen."

That explains it, thought Castle to himself. Explains just about anything the kid would do.

"Has he gone missing?"

"No. I mean yes. Well sort of."

"I see."

"He left home."

"They'll do that, that age."

"But I don't know where he has gone to."

"When was the last time you saw Billy?"

"Last night. Or, rather, yesterday evening about six o'clock."

"Well if it has been less than twenty-four hours…"

"He drives by the house in a roadster with a girl at his side."

Lucky boy, Castle thought. A roadster at his age. Me, I'm long past seventeen, and I got an old Nash. Two months I have mine out of storage, and they go and slap on gas rationing.

"I don't quite understand the problem, ma'am?"

"Driving by the house like that. It is as if he is taunting me."

"Why would he do such a thing? Did he leave the house in a huff?"

"No, this is so unlike him. He was always, I mean, he has always been such a kind and considerate boy."

"Did he have the roadster before he left home yesterday? Or did he just buy it?"

"Yes. I mean, he didn't just buy the roadster. And he didn't leave home yesterday, it was nearly a year ago."

"He left home a year ago in his roadster, drives by the house but never rings the bell."

"Yes, I wave from the window or come rushing out the front door but he drives away. The pretty young girl by his side. Billy keeps his eyes on the road but the girl looks back and smiles."

"Have you ever taken down the number on his plate?"

"No. I can never see it well enough."

"Do you drive a car, Mrs. Myerhoff? Have you tried to follow him? Has your husband?"

"I don't have a car and my husband, he passed away three years ago. Billy was just fourteen then, nearly fifteen."

"So you want me to find Billy?"

"Yes. Please do. Tell him to come visit his mother who loves him."

Mrs. Myerhoff opened her handbag, brought out a wrinkled handerchief and held it to her nose. Castle always thought of offering his own handkerchief in these situations. Not that these situations occurred too often but the bit with the handkerchief was always being performed by gallant gentlemen in motion pictures. He never followed through for fear that his handkerchief might be dirty, the woman'd look at it, make a face.

"You realize, of course, I cannot force him to come to visit you."

"Yes, I realize that. Just let me know how he is and tell him that I love him."

"Yes, ma'am. It'll be thirty dollars a day and I have to charge expenses, gas money, if necessary, on account of rationing."

Mrs. Myerhoff opened the handbag that she'd just closed, fished in her purse, brought out the wrinkled bills, leaned forward and placed them in a mosaiced ashtray.

"I just don't know where it goes these days," Mrs. Myerhoff said. "No sooner do you get it than you spend it. Hardly enough left for me to go do my shopping on Hastings Street."

Castle nodded his head with what he hoped was convincing and resigned acceptance of this quotidian truth.

Then, weary with making that pretense, he considered the mosaic ashtrays. He had four of them on his big oak desk, each made by a different acquaintance who'd done time at the Penitentiary in New Westminster. Guys got out, they brought Castle an ashtray.

He always hated the money part. Hated to have to raise his daily rate by five bucks. It was always sordid no matter how the dough was exchanged. It looked especially tawdry now, the dull paper money lying across the colourful bits of tile.

Castle couldn't bring himself to take the money out of the ashtray. He left it there and wrote down Mrs. Myerhoff's address.

"I'll find him for you," Castle said, as he escorted her across the office and around the Chinese screen. "Don't worry about that."

She looked at him curiously.

"You will?"

"Yes, I will."

Mrs. Myerhoff didn't reply, just looked at him, and the corners of her mouth twisted down. Castle wondered what exactly that signified as he opened the door for her. He stood watching after her until she reached the staircase, then he closed the door, glanced at his alias from this side of the frosted glass:

GENE CASTLE

9 - 2

Chapter Three

Castle had been looking forward to a quiet morning with the *Encyclopedia Britannica.* Maybe have a little tipple around eleven o'clock. He'd been on volume fifteen for years. Not that he was such a slow reader; there was always something to intervene, usually a war or a minor revolution. Of course, he had idled away spare hours during the past year, when there was no work and Louise was off displaying her assets to the doughboys, with other reading matter, mainly *Ring Magazine* and a hundred-year-old medical textbook. There had, as well, been a brief trip to France but that was another story.

There was nothing for it but to trudge back down the stairs, make a couple of phone calls. This thing should be easy enough to wrap up. Easier if whoever it was that owned the Standard Building would have phone lines installed in the offices.

Laura's sweet voice with its tender lilt flitted around the marble lobby, as she told whoever on the other end of the line that, no, she wouldn't meet him after work for a drink at the Manhattan Club even if he was the last man on the goddamned planet and anyway her boyfriend owned the goddamned Manhattan Club so what do you think of them apples you peanut-prick son-of-a-whore!

"I hope," Castle said, "that wasn't a would-be customer of mine."

"Yeah, and the hell with you too, bub!"

Laura yanked a wire out of a hole and shoved it in somewhere else. She looked fierce so Castle decided it was best to go about his business of using the telephone in the booth by the entrance. He sat on the wooden stool waiting for the revolving doors to revolve and for Danny Bartoli to answer, wondering whether Bartoli would be cool to him because of the look that passed between them that morning.

The Detective picked up and Castle announced himself, didn't notice any hostility when Bartoli said, "How ya, doin?"

"I want to prevail upon you to run down a vehicle registration number for me."

One thing about Danny, he wasn't the sort to waste time reminding him that it was against procedure, that he wasn't supposed to do anything like that, and that he could get in trouble. Either do it or don't do it, was the way both of them thought.

"Okay, but I'll need a couple of hours."

"Thanks, Danny. You can leave the message with the hot-tempered young lady at the switchboard."

Castle hung up and battled his way out of the booth.

"Hey, Gene!"

"Yeah, Laura," Castle answered, taking a defensive stance, hands up in front of his face.

"I'm sorry for snapping at you."

"That's okay. I'm used to your moody ways. Say, are you and Art Sprague really back together?"

"Naw, I just told the jerk that. Once it's over, it's over. You know what I mean? No, you wouldn't. You're a one woman man and, as you very well know, Art's got a crush on that woman. And, you know who I got a crush on though I'm on the lookout nevertheless. Yeah, so all in all, it's a crazy mixed up world."

"Out of the mouths of babes. Now, Laura your happiness is always on my mind so a little word to the wise here. A guy's going to call me in a couple of hours with a bit of info. I probably won't be around so you can chat him up and who knows. They tell me the dames think he is a bit of all right. Name of Danny Bartoli."

"Yeah, and what's he do?"

"He's a cop. A Detective. We met on account of…"

"On account of he's a cop."

"Yeah, I shot his uncle once."

"And he likes you?"

"Better'n he likes his uncle. You consider going out with a cop?"

"I never have before but I'm getting desperate."

"Reminds me of a dame Louise was telling me about. Name of Trixie Nicks. She used to… well, never mind."

"Yeah, well, I didn't used to, didn't used to have to but I'm getting used to it now."

"Well, I'd like to stay and hear more but I'm working."

Castle went out onto Pender Street where it wasn't raining. It hadn't rained for nearly thirty-six hours. He headed west, keeping on the north side of the street. Castle never crossed to the south side until he was at least a block away in either direction. He couldn't bear walking past the intersection of Pender and little Shanghai Alley, the scene of so much excitement and sadness in the past. Of course, if he was going avoid streets with sadness or excitement attached to them he'd probably have to move somewhere on the west side of town, way west, maybe out by the University, nothing ever happens out there. Take an office on a street with a lot of trees on it, where the doctors and lawyers and guys who ran forestry companies lived. They had the trees over there on the west side whereas the guys who cut down the trees lived on the east side of town and didn't have trees. Come to think of it those west side guys owned the houses and transient hotels on the east side where you found the bush apes. The west side guys probably had all the trees cut down to do the workers a favour. You got sick of trees out in the bush. The big capitalists were considerate that way. They were being even more considerate starting this brand new war, put people back to work. Even women were working. They might have started a war a few years ago. Jumped into the thing in Spain, stopped Hitler before he hardly got started but being considerate, they waited, the capitalists did. Hell, Castle told himself, those humanitarians knew that it would only have taken a few months to put paid to the paperhanger's ambitions but what then? You give people jobs for those precious few months and then sign a treaty, send them back to relief camps? Yeah, sure. Some of our boys are going to die but what glorious deaths those will be. In the cause of freedom and democracy, don't you know. Not to mention the economy. You can't let Death stand in the way of Progress. If the people let that happen then, well, take automobiles for instance. What if we had listened to the sage who pointed out back in 1890-something that automobiles would crash into other automobiles or into trees or into people walking down the street minding their own business? You can not manufacture automobiles and let them run around hell's acre because hundreds, thousands, millions of people will be killed. Where would we be then, for chrissakes?

Jesus! Castle was at Burrard Street before he snapped out of it. His mind surfaced from wherever it had gone to rant and rave, and he found himself staring at the Vancouver Hotel, up at the Rooftop Garden, with the Palomar Ballroom across the way, each of them a home for the kind of music that caused Harry 'the Hipster' Heinz to run when he heard it, stick a needle in his arm. And that he, Gene Castle, didn't dig either. Nevertheless, there were people who insisted on calling it jazz. Hot jazz, no less.

Robson Street and the library were a short block away. He went in and right off saw the balding librarian with the bow tie, saw the gent clear his throat to get the attention of the female librarian who wore her hair in a bun as female librarians must have been required to do. Castle, a past master of the art of lip reading, watched in his peripheral vision the gent saying, "Here he is!"

Her lips forming a sound like, "Oh, pshaw!" Her blushing slightly.

"He's even more weathered than the last time," Bowtie said. "If that's possible."

Not wishing to interrupt their discussion, Castle located the 1939 city directory all by himself and discovered the curious, to him, information that N. Myerhoff was listed as the sole resident at her digs up on Fraser Street near 34 Avenue. There was a Rodney Myerhoff living at 682 Jackson Street; maybe, Castle thought, a relative of the deceased husband. Things got curiouser when he checked the 1938 city directory. Seems that Rodney was living on Fraser Street that year. He had been there in 1937 and 1936, and there was one other Myerhoff in residence in 1935, a 'W.' Which could have been long for Billy. 'W' was part of the household all the way back to 1929 which marked the first appearance of anyone named Myerhoff in Vancouver.

Castle closed the books and stared off in the direction of the Religion section. Mrs. Myerhoff had obviously been so upset by her visit to his office that she'd gotten her dates all mixed up. You had a hotrod kid driving around with his doxie taunting his dear old mum, it could get to you, if you were the dear old mum. That had to be the reason for the discrepancy because otherwise the mix-up in the dates made no sense whatsoever.

Assuming that 'W' did indicate the boy and not Rodney's sister Willahmina or his brother Walter, it meant the son must have been maintaining a separate residence since 1935. Trouble was, Mrs. Myerhoff gave her son's age as eighteen which meant he would have been wheeling his roadster around town, living on his own, since he was thirteen.

Then there was the question of the husband. That didn't add up. She said he'd been killed three years ago, which would have been 1937 but he was listed in the 1938 directory. And was in the current directory but at a different address. So, perhaps, she had made an understandable mistake with the date and just by coincidence another Rodney Myerhoff shows up on Jackson Street.

Castle broke off staring and sighed. Just when I thought I'd be earning some easy money. Just when I thought I'd have a beer at the Seaman's Club while waiting for Danny Bartoli to call me back, so's I can wrap this up in one day, get back to my encyclopedia, feet up on the desk in my lovely office, have a taste of rye whiskey, wait for Louise to get back to the Rose Hotel, where I'd have another taste—it all gets complicated.

Poor Mrs. Myerhoff with her handbag and her purse, her worn Hudson's Bay basement lightweight coat, a lost soul.

Castle got up and started toward the religion section. He noticed that the little fellow with the bowtie was standing near the shelves in his path. The man glanced over at the lady librarian at her desk, as if for help. Then he asked Castle if he could help him. He had a hard time getting it out, the poor man. The first time, nothing happened, he opened his mouth and closed it like he needed a big gulp of air. Then the second time it came out in a strangled mutter.

"Yeah," Castle said. "I'm looking for a book on saints."

"S-saints?"

"Yeah, you know. Saints."

The guy went to the shelves, found a thick book, handed it to Castle with a tight little smile.

"I'm looking for the patron saint of Lost Souls."

"Oh," said the bowtie.

"You wouldn't happen to know who that is, would you?"

"No. No sir."

Castle thumbed through the book, bowtie still standing there though he'd backed up a step or two.

"Saint Afra," Castle said. "Of Augsburg."

The guy nodded his head.

"You know," Castle said, peering closely at him. "You

42

remind me of a guy I shot once in Nicaragua."

"I…you did?"

"Yeah, but not before he taught me to read lips."

"Oh, I. You do? I didn't mean…"

"Tell your lady friend I may be weathered but she'd get used to it."

"Oh, yes. Indeed, I… I will."

Castle handed him the book and left the library.

He hoofed it back to the east side of town where he felt more comfortable, going directly to the garage between Hastings and Pender Street where he kept his 1932 Nash. It being a doughty four-door sedan, Castle told himself he'd have to quell his desire to have a race with Roadster Billy, if he ever found him.

The guy with the toque and the face like mashed potatoes was sitting on a stool in front of the entrance like he'd been doing ever since Castle could remember. The guy made a gesture with thumb and forefinger, in the vicinity of his forehead, like he always did. It was as if he was remembering old hats he used to have, tugging at brims of times past.

Castle walked to the rear of the garage. He kept the Nash at the back—not so much to be inconspicuous but because he was a considerate fellow, despite his reputation to the contrary; no sense being in the middle of the automotive action if you were only a sporadic participant. Maybe there was some kind of civic award he could apply for.

He muscled the monster out of the garage, down the alley and over to Hastings Street where he noticed Twinkle-toes Feinstein engaged in a vigourous conversation with Double Jimmy. The two went way back. T-Toes had been a hoofer for many years before he got too old for Vaudeville, and took up with Double Jimmy (real name, James James) —who was the kind of guy who gave fight managers a bad name. But he was also, as he freely admitted, innovative. Double Jimmy hired T-

Toes to work with his boys, teach them to move, to dance. Last guy they worked together with was Renny Weeks, nephew of Raymond Thomas. The kid danced his way to twelve straight victories and then he ran into Sammy Menoza who cut in on his record, knocking him to the dance floor nine times during their brutal rendezvous. It was a dance from which Renny never recovered. Renny being now a 26-year-old punch drunk custodian, and that only through Gene Castle's intervention with the representative of the owner of the Standard Building.

Yeah, Castle thought, maybe they'll give me a humanitarian prize, go with the considerate parking garage client award.

Castle crossed the Cambie Street Bridge, headed for the wastelands south of Broadway. Made Fraser Street, saw block after block of homes—if you looked at them from the air, a little biplane type thing cruising around, on the lookout for German bombers, all these streets with little houses might remind you of the inside of a waffle iron. At least that's what they'd remind Castle of, should he ever be up in an airplane looking down.

Nora Myerhoff's joint was like all the rest of them. Little bungalow, little lawn. He was willing to bet that all the hydrangeas and all the bay laurel hedges were related. We've taken over this part of town, you California lilacs, you damned rhododendrons, stay the hell out of South Vancouver, keep to your own turf, over there on the west side of town.

Mrs. Myerhoff had said she'd be shopping on Hastings Street. She'd probably call at Save-On Meats, Woodwards before taking the streetcar home, so he could poke around undisturbed. He gave the place a slant, told himself to circle the block, then asked himself why he used the word 'circle'; afterall the block was a rectangle; he answered himself by saying it wouldn't sound right, telling himself to "rectangle the block."

When he and his self were finished their talk, Castle pulled up in the laneway, beside the garage at the back of Mrs. Myerhoff's house. He got out and peeked in the side window.

Nothing in there except boxes and jars on shelves; some garden tools leaning in a corner, looking like they hadn't been in manly hands for some time, what with all the cobwebs—or in unmanly hands for that matter.

Castle continued around to the street, parked, turned off the engine, got out and knocked on the nextdoor neighbour's door. When no one answered, he knocked on the other nextdoor neighbour's door. An ample lady in a robe answered. The top of her slip was visible above her robe. Faded blue frilly fringe. He could smell the booze. She gave him the onceover.

"I'm sorry to bother you, madam. I'm looking for Rodney Myerhoff."

"You got the wrong house, bub. Though he's been in this house, a time or two. You'd have gone nextdoor that would have been the wrong house too, even when he was living there."

"He's an old friend of mine, Rodney."

"He is, eh?"

"You know, from the old days. Thought I'd look him up. You have any idea where he might have gone?"

"Yeah, you might say, he went back to the old days."

"How do you mean?"

"Rod was the kind of guy liked to have a drink, a good time, and he wasn't getting either nextdoor. Wasn't getting anything over there, you get my meaning."

"So, he left the old lady, eh?"

"Yeah, went to live closer to the action. He still does a circuit of the joints."

"You remind me of a lady, likes a bit of action yourself. Hell you doing living out here in the sticks?"

"Married my big butter and egg man only he had a massive coronary thrombosis. Ernestine Brady's my name. Yours?"

She held out a plump hand, rings on several short fingers. He shook it, her hand was warm and moist. She might not have been bad looking before the butter and eggs.

He told her his name.

"So, Gene. I bet you wouldn't be offended I offered you a wee drink. Why don't you come on back to the kitchen, park yourself on a chair and help me while away a beautiful day in June?"

"Well, Ernestine…"

"Let's not beat around the bush, Gene. We're both adults, eh? I kind of got a yen for a little adventure."

Ernestine pretended to let her robe fall open by mistake, and Castle saw her slip was really a sort of teddy that barely covered her hips. Her legs were pretty good, if a trifle plump near the top.

"I'm good at it," Ernestine said.

"Oh, I bet you are."

"Well?"

"Well, you see, I got a date downtown, Ernestine."

She closed her robe quicker than she'd opened it, smirked at him.

Castle told her so-long and started down the stairs, turned back, "They had a kid, didn't they?"

She nodded.

"Billy. Nice boy. His daddy bought him a '32 Ford Roadster for his eighteenth birthday. Crashed it the day after he got his driver's license. He was killed. Him and his girl friend. It was a shame."

"Yeah."

"You come back some time, Gene. I'm lonely."

Castle got in the Nash, hit the starter button and pulled away. Yeah, the world is full of lonely people. Ernestine Brady and Nora Myerhoff, living cheek to jowl, each an entirely different sort of woman but both of them lonely. Even if everyone else on the block had their social calendars booked up for the duration, the two together made for a lot of loneliness in one neighbourhood. Multiply that by all the neighbourhoods in the city and…well, enough of that.

He made the trip back downtown wondering about poor

Mrs. Myerhoff, why she would send him on an errand like this, lie about her child and her husband.

He left the Nash in the garage and headed back to the Standard Building. Laura must have seen him out of the corner of her eye or else sensed him, because she reached for a pink slip of paper, waved it in the air without looking at him, continued talking into her mouthpiece, yanking at wires. Castle leaned against the Dutch door to ponder the significance of the message. It expressed Henry the Hipster's wish that Castle would fall by the Neon Angel that evening, and, the jivecat affirmed, he was "serious."

It wasn't so much that the message was significant but that he had gotten a message at all. Laura had two little pieces of pine with spikes sticking out of them. One contained messages for Beanie Brown, the bookie; the other spike easily took care of the rest of the people in the building.

"So," Laura said, turning away from her work. "Where you been?"

"Took the Nash out for a spin. Figure I ought to do that every year or so."

"Nash? I thought you had a Plymouth."

"I traded my nine-year-old Plymouth for an eight-year-old Nash."

"Went out with a guy a couple of years ago, had a Nash."

"Maybe that's the very one I bought on account of mine has a rip in the headliner over the backseat."

"You figure I'd be offended but I'm not."

Laura started another sentence but stopped, looked just above the bottom half of the Dutch door and just to the left of Castle's left arm, and made a sound like "Hmmmm."

"What?" Castle asked without turning around.

"Get a load of him."

"Hey, Gene," a voice called.

"Danny. How's it going?"

"Introduce me," Laura muttered. "Introduce me."

Danny Bartoli came up to the door and he and Castle shook hands. Castle made the introduction and stood back to watch. Laura fixed her blue eyes on him, or in him, and Bartoli blushed right through his complexion that was the colour of Ovaltine. Then, embarrassed by his reaction, Bartoli got a cocky expression on his face as if women looked at him that way all the time.

"I have the information you wanted."

He glanced back at Laura who was still staring at him, little lights going off unheeded on her board. Castle noticed the way Bartoli slitted his eyes doing it.

"Laura," Castle said. "Those are probably important calls for me that you're ignoring."

She gave him a dirty look but turned to her board.

Castle indicated to Bartoli that they should move to another part of the lobby. The Detective followed him but couldn't help look over his shoulder at Laura.

"The broad's…"

"Yeah, Danny. I know."

Castle not liking the way he said it. Then thinking, what am I, jealous?

"Yeah. Anyway. What you wanted me to look up. There's no vehicle registered to anybody in this town named Myerhoff. A fellow named Rodney Myerhoff used to have a 1932 Ford Roadster but he hasn't owed it since 1937 which was when a William Myerhoff ran it off West Marine Drive, bounced it off a tree and rolled it down an embankment. It being a vehicle with no roof to protect anyone inside, you can imagine what was inside wasn't too pleasant."

"What was inside?"

"Since I figured you wanted more than names, I looked up the file because I'm a good friend…"

"And may need a favour some day."

"That too, of course. William Myerhoff, age 18 was killed but not killed as bad as his passenger, Florence, uh, let me check my notes."

Bartoli got his notebook out of the inside breast pocket of his suit jacket, wet an index finger and flicked through the pages.

"Yeah, she was no Florence Nightingale, that's for sure. Florence Dolman, also 18, a professional girl."

"Dolman? Oh, shit. Little Flo."

"You knew her?"

"Yeah, but not in a commercial sense. She was a regular at Ramona's a few years ago. I always wondered what happened to her."

"What happened to her wasn't pretty. Her head was not found inside the car with the rest of her. It was found at the top of the hill the car rolled down."

Castle shook his head at the picture of it.

"Yeah, it gets worse. Florence, Flo, you called her, was a working girl which explains another part of it. She was working at the time of the accident. Her work was so good that it probably caused the accident."

"You mean she was…?"

"Yeah, because when the car hit the tree, she had to have bitten if off and then the car rolled and decapitated her. It was still in her mouth when they found her head."

"I hope to hell no one told this to the parents."

"Both sets of parents, what they were told was he lost control of the vehicle. The kid's parents, they were pretty broken up, it says. The girl's parents, they lived in Merritt, they didn't ask any questions, just said, 'Okay.'"

"Okay. It is not pleasant information but thanks for it and let me know how I have to make it even with you."

"You already did," the Detective said, and nodded his head in the direction of Laura at the switchboard. "I want to get me a little bit of that."

Castle didn't like the way he said that either.

He walked out onto the street with Danny Bartoli but refused his offer of a ride. The Detective gave him a knowing look, based around a wry twist of the mouth, a look that acknowledged the fact that Castle didn't want to be seen around town with a cop.

Castle headed for the Seaman's Club which was over Goody's Goods, a store owned by an old friend of his father's and that catered to men who worked in the bush and on the boats. The Club was private, for men who'd been to sea. Castle qualified because he spent many a winter shipping out while other carnies were holed up at winter quarters. He'd called at Maracaibo and Paramariabo, The Bay of Biscay and the Bight of Benin. But he was just a callow cabin boy compared with some of the salts who huddled telling stories at little round tables covered with oilcloth.

The place was at its best in the winter when the rain was rattling the windows, or in the spring and fall when the rain was doing the same thing, not at the beginning of summer when you could possibly look outside at sunshine, and it wasn't intimate somehow. No, you needed rain and the oil stove fired up, the smell of kerosene burning; then you could listen close while Matty Muldoon or Rufus Kilkenny, his heir apparent, told stories. At any other gathering of men like this anywhere else in the world, Rufus Kilkenny would be the main man. But you could bet no other gathering of such men had a Matty Muldoon in its midst. There was no truth to the story that Matty had shipped with Captain Vancouver but he was closing in on his ninetieth year and had been to every port in the world long before there was a city named for the Captain.

Kilkenny still went to sea, albeit on Canadian Pacific passenger ships plying the Pacific—still went to sea despite being seventy-two years old and having one leg. He was between trips now, over in a corner by himself, scribbling in his journals. Kilkenny had shown his journal to Castle once, or shown him one black and white speckled volume of hundreds. He kept account of all his experiences at sea, included crude sketches and pasted in postcards of his ports of call, as well as photographs of himself and his mates taken throughout the world.

So Castle sat there in the afternoon sunlight nursing the double Navy Rum that he'd wanted in the morning, staring at motes of dust. He thought of Paris, what it would be like right now, today, with guys in jackboots and gray uniforms marching along the Boulevards, prowling about the narrow streets. Thought of that little place off rue des Bernardins, a little three-storey hotel, his room on the top floor whenever he was in Paris; he could look out the window and down on the little park with the statue of Francois Villon, of all people.

"Why so melancholy, chum?"

Castle glanced up but not too far up at Joe Frontenac, indicated the other chair, and the reporter sat down.

"I was thinking of Paris, Joe, which is where we ought to be. Especially a guy like you. You ought to be sending back one of your inimitable stories about the fall of Paris, the exodus."

"You're right about that, and what am I doing instead? Hanging around this burg, hoping inspiration'll strike."

"What about Treherne?"

"I already wrote it. What a story to tell and what a story I told. Pretty good job, if I do say so myself."

"So what's the problem?"

"The next one."

"Oh."

"Guess I'll have to do something impressionistic, you know a sort of celebration of the streets. Street life."

"You mean, a kind of hymn to the hum and the hustle."

"Yeah, a prose poem thing. Just record what passes in front of my eyes. A poor woman looking in the window. A freckled tyke rolling a barrel hoop. A hooker leaning against a brick wall under a red light, down at the end of Shanghai Alley, the light making a veil around her head."

"A bloody veil."

"Hey, that's not bad."

"Thanks."

"Saw a tough-looking little guy the other day, Jewish guy I

think. Maybe a fighter. It was raining, he had his hat pulled down low and he was trying to like a cigarette."

"John Garfield standing in the rain. The tyke is Mickey Rooney a few years back. The old lady, I don't know, Marjorie Main. The hooker, just like Bette Davis. Yeah, you write your whatever you call it, prose poem, and all the people in it could be movie actors. Just hope you can find a Dolores Del Rio."

"Me, too. I just might do that."

"Don't forget my percentage."

"Right. So what's on your mind?"

"I'm thinking about a woman whose son got killed but she pretends he's still alive."

"Trying to figure why she does it?"

"No, I know why she does it."

"Yeah, it is a tough world."

"Yeah," Castle said. He made a gesture with his thumb, jabbing it over his shoulder like he was an umpire calling out a baserunner. "Ask that guy about that. Come to think of it, there's another column. You ought to be a busy guy for awhile."

He told Frontenac a little bit about Rufus Kilkenny, and the reporter thanked him. "I guess I owe you, again."

"Uh huh, I guess you do. Oh, and Rufus has a wooden leg."

"How'd he lose it?"

"He was on some islands, Sulawesi, I think it was. This was in the aughts, and he was captured by pirates. They have these curved knives called Pangas. Cut off his leg, bit by bit. Sawed right through the bone."

Frontenac shook his head in wonder.

"Don't see much of that sort of thing around here."

"I don't know about that," Castle replied. "Guess it depends on where you hang out."

CHAPTER FOUR

He finished his drink, introduced the reporter to the old salt and left them alone.

Out on the street, Castle thought about folding himself into a phone booth, calling Mrs. Myerhoff, or driving out to see her but he couldn't face it. There was no job to do, after all. Maybe he ought to just mail the money back to her. Keep a fin back for expenses. Still, he was curious about the husband. Why would she pretend he was dead? Well, later for that. He had an appointment back at his office with an old companion in whose company he could be comfortable, put his feet up on the desk, have a sip of his own rum. Maybe when seven o'clock rolled around he'd turn on his radio set, listen to the Voice of Doom. His old friend was the *Encyclopedia Britannica* (Coronation Edition), volume fifteen, 'Maryb to Mushe.' They hadn't gotten together in almost a year but Castle remembered where they'd left off. He had been moving in on 'Moloch.'

Castle could hardly wait. He hot-footed it back to the Standard Building through busy streets of patriots.

It was ten at night before Castle came down from his office. By then he knew all about Moloch, that scary king-like figure who was making vengeful long before there was an old testament. The only way to appease that fanatic was to sacrifice your children. Moloch had a big appetite for children.

After reading that, Castle had been in no mood for Moltke so went on to Mom, who wasn't the dear sweet lady who'd turn around from the oven when you came crashing through the Saturday afternoon screendoor hungry from ball-playing, who'd wipe her hands on her apron, bring the hot cherry pie to the table, cut you a slice, set down a glass of milk, wet her finger and press the cowlick down on your tousled real boy's head of hair.

Everybody's Mom.

Yeah, just like mine, Castle thought grimly.

No, the Mom he was thinking about was a written sign language used by some people in the Cameroons. He wondered if there was a sign in Mom for Mom. Maybe a stick figure whacking a smaller stick figure across the side of the head, her other hand holding a glass of gin.

He was on Carrall Street, crossing the alley halfway down the hill to Hastings when the lights hit, half blinding him. He made out two shadows on the periphery and then the shadows became figures, and he recognized them as Koronicki and Bartoli, only they weren't wearing their half-friendly let's-keep-in-touch-with-our-favourite-denizen-of-the-streets expression. They had on normal cop faces.

"What's this about?"

"It is about the bindle stiff we found murdered on Hastings Street today," Koronicki said.

"The Professor. What're we going to do, make a campfire in the alley, sit around it and sing some of his old songs?"

"No," the Chief shook his head. "We're gonna ask you a question about him."

Castle glanced from the Chief to Bartoli, who looked back with the hard-eye. Not too many hours ago, we'd been sort of like buddies. I was even sort of a matchmaker. Cops. You can't ever really trust them.

"So, ask."

"How come he had your name on a slip of paper in the chest pocket of his shirt?"

"You mean why in the chest pocket of his shirt instead of, say, the back pocket of his pants?"

"Don't get smart with us, Castle," Bartoli said.

"So now it's Castle, eh?"

"Yeah," said Koronicki. "You got any answer for my question?"

"No, I don't. Like I told you this morning, I knew the man, liked him, respected him. Hell, I even looked up to him and guys like him. I haven't seen him in years. Maybe he knew he was going to be in Vancouver and made a note to himself to look me up. Talk about old times. He knew my old man too. That's all I can tell you."

"No, you can tell us another thing."

"Maybe."

"Who do you know with the initials 'L. M.'?"

Castle stood there staring at Koronicki while in his mind going through a catalogue of friends and acquaintances. A rogues' gallery, one after another turning over like one of those signs with advertisements such as you see attached to clocks in restaurants.

He was about to say that he couldn't think of anyone he knew with those initials but then he remembered one. "Leon Mandrake. Only one I can think of."

"The magician?"

"Yeah."

"He knew Treherne?"

"I don't know."

Then Castle thought of another 'L. M.' but he sure as hell wasn't going to mention this fellow.

"When was the last time you saw the Great Mandrake?"

"Couple of years ago."

"You sure?"

"Sure, I'm sure. Why?"

"Well, on the slip of paper we found, between your name and the initials, there was the word 'for'."

"The number four?"

"No. How it read was: 'Gene Castle—for L. M.' How do you explain that?"

"I don't."

They ran out of questions so they just stared at him with those looks they must have to study at the Police Academy. Castle tried to picture it. Guys going to the front of the class, one by one, practicing on the professor. Guy flunking out, having to go home and explain to the townsfolk down to the general store: Boys, I just didn't have the look. These two, Koronicki and Bartoli, had the look.

When they were done giving it, they got into the unmarked and drove away.

Castle continued his walk to the Rose Hotel where, hopefully, Louise would be waiting.

From a second-floor room on Hastings Street, a radio could be heard through a window open on a warm late June evening. A tenor saxophone was playing with the melody of "Ain't Nobody's Business." Yeah, he thought, nobody's but cops. Damned Leandro Martine, he added.

The next morning, Louise beat the blues, was out of the room and the hotel and off to rehearsal before Castle got out of bed. By the time he'd had a whore's bath, the guy was across the street singing about the little girl he'd lost.

Castle raised the green shade and saw Cordova Street all bustling under a sky like watery white paint brushed over a base of pale blue. He stood looking down at the action, women with lunch buckets, old men out for their morning stroll, kids manoeuvring between them. One man was standing by the door of his radio repair shop with a broom in his hands, scratching his head, waiting for a break in the traffic so he could take lick at the sidewalk.

Castle thought back to being a kid on the streets. His adventures had taken him to this very same block back in another era entirely. It was a whole universe down there, the universe of the streets. Everybody in the neighbourhood was connected somehow. The working man, the hustler, the housewife or wartime working girl, the old lady on the wooden steps, the tout who rented a room at the top of the stairs. Remove one and the universe was affected.

"Little girl, little girl, where have you gone…?"

If that little girl was as fantastic as the man claimed, she must have caused some changes in her neighbourhood. Think of the men hanging out on the corner. Their loss some other corner's gain.

Castle didn't want to go to work. For a minute, thinking about that racetrack tout, he figured he had his excuse. But, no, it being Tuesday, the track was closed. What's a man to do? He was a shirker that's what he was. He'd hit the streets and shirk his responsibilities.

He went across the street, wanting to start a conversation with the blues man. At first, the guy regarded him with suspicion. Then they discovered they had at least one friend in common: Sam Case who used to play trumpet at the Porters' Retreat. But it wasn't enough to break down the man's reserve.

"Haven't see Sam around in awhile," Castle said.

"No, Sam, he's with Eddie Adderson's band, travelling the country. Oh, yeah."

The man wasn't brown, he really was black. Had that patch over his left eye, some white in his close cropped hair, white in the hair you could see above his top button.

"You wouldn't be the white man was a friend to the giant?"

"The giant?"

"Yeah, you know, big fellow worked at the Retreat, never said nothing."

"You must be talking about Abel Hibbs."

"Yeah, Abel. Big sweet fellow."

"I knew Abel for over twenty years. We used to travel together."

"Well, all right then."

The black man took his hand from the belly of the guitar and offered it to Castle. His fingers were like garter snakes.

"Deep South," the man said. "Deep South Durkins."

"Gene Castle."

"Yeah. I like that."

"What? My name?"

"Shit," the man grinned. "No. I like you didn't ask me about my name. You know, like, 'How you get your name? You from the deep south?'"

"You didn't ask me how I got mine either. 'You from a castle?'"

Durkins laughed, did some business on the guitar.

"Yeah, I'm from way down in the middle of M'ssippi. 'Bout twenty year ago, I come up to Portland on a train."

"You had a cushion seat?"

"Not in this lifetime, brother. Sidedoor pullman. Met some boys in Portland."

"They gave you your moniker?"

"Oh, lord. You done rode the trains youself."

"Sure did."

"So, these boys were making fun of my accent and my big old country shoes. Told them I was from down there hard by Eupora, they say, 'You deep south, gates.' So I been Deep South ever since. Good friends, though, they call me South. You can call me South."

"All right, South. You can call me Castle."

"I met another white fellow the other day but I met him before. Long ago. Another knight of the road. Funny old bo.

Can't hardly talk to you without making a rhyme of it. Says to me: 'Hi there South, open your mouth, tap your shoes, sing some of them blues.'"

Castle laughed, "Well, I'll be damned. There's only one person that can be. He a chubby kind of fellow, always smiling?"

"That's the man."

"Wears a John B. Stetson hat?"

"All the time."

"High-Line Mason."

"Uh huh. I met him in Kansas City," South said. "Way back before the last war."

"So, he's in town?"

"Was last week. He jungled up over there near all those tracks and factories. Big old street over there."

"Terminal Avenue?"

"Sounds like it."

"Maybe I'll look him up soon. I got to go now, South."

"Whatchew up to?"

"I'm slacking, malingering."

"That's good. That's good."

Castle started off and Deep South Durkins began picking out "Lazy Bones."

He had breakfast at Ramona's and read the *Times*, every word of it, turning first to Frontenac's 'I Was There' column about Professor Treherne. When he was finished that, he hit the streets and had coffee at another place, read the entire *Herald*, as well as the weekly rag out of Burnaby. There was most of a *Seattle Post* that some traveler had left but who the hell wanted to read about that dreary burg?

Castle walked east to Jackson, a street with wooden staircases and no trees. He climbed a rickety set to Myerhoff's aparment but no one answered his knocking. He shrugged his shoulders and pretended to be disappointed.

Castle's next stop was a newstand where he bought *Ring Magazine* and went through it on a bench in Victory Square. Every once in a while he looked up from the magazine and over at three Indian men who were sprawled on the grass, drinking from a paper bag. They were laughing and goofing with each other when Castle first sat down and they were asleep when he got up.

He walked to Granville Street, staying on Hastings so that he never passed within a block of his office. He turned south on Granville and up ahead saw The Strand Theatre. The showcard near the ticket booth featured Clark Gable snuggled up to Hedy Lamarr. The film was called 'Comrade X.' Well, what the hell, Castle thought, he'd go in, forget about the war and about kids in car crashes, lonely mothers and lonely nextdoor neighbours in satin slips.

Hedy Lamarr, there's someone he'd like to see in a satin slip. Or in the same knee high boots, she's wearing in this silly movie. It is set in and around Moscow only they're using the same sets so familiar from movies about New York. And then there are scenes where Gable and Lamarr and her father, what's his name, usually in Westerns, usually the immigrant home-steader who you knew was going to get attacked by Indians soon as they got up from drinking in the park, Felix Bressart—they're fleeing in a tank from an entire tank corps, heading for the Romanian border, and the hills are the same Southern California hills where they shoot westerns.

Anyway, Gable's a foreign correspondant, one of many in Moscow, but the Commissar of Propaganda, Oscar Homolka, has his knickers in a knot because one of the reporters is a spy, Comrade X. Of course, this is Gable who you are supposed to think is nothing more than a wastrel, drinking his way through his tour of duty, but he's really a Scarlet Pimpernel sort of a guy and wins the heart of Hedy, the strong-willed trolley driver and dedicated Party member. And there's nothing wrong with her that a nice outfit, a hotdog and a trip to Ebbets Field in Brooklyn won't cure. But the thing that made Castle angry all through the thing and as he walked out onto the streets was the goddamned Yankee attitude of it all, the all-furrners-are-idiotic-children aspect. Not only that, it bothered him the Soviet Union was the enemy. Here, they were fighting the Nazis—but they're blustering nincompoops, not to be taken seriously; it's the Reds the Yankees are concerned about. Which is why they'd be staying out of this war unless someone came and whacked them over the head.

Hell, he didn't want any part of it, either, but for different reasons.

What he wanted was a drink.

You got to the Manhattan Club by climbing a set of spavined stairs that were on the other side of a door heavy with decades of paint, the door set in a brick wall between stores that were directly across Hastings Street from a big seahorse that hovered over the pavement and announced the Only Seafood Restaurant, third oldest business in the city, an entire year younger than Ramona's, and two years junior to the Seven Little Tailors.

You had to be tough to climb those stairs. There were only fourteen of them but you could read entire sordid and sorry histories during the climb between the ground floor door and the one at the top of stairs. There were dollops of sloppy paint and drops of blood and along the walls, smudges made by greasy heads before the person underneath took a header at four in the afternoon or four in the morning. Maybe the person just rested the head against the wall and stayed there, unable to take another step, not moving even when some other person came scampering up the same staircase, hot for action. Castle figured if he ever got brave enough to lean his own head, the side of his head, against the walls, he'd be able to hear lost conversations, shouts, endearments, curses and imprecations. Castle was not unaware that illicit sexual congress occurred on these stairs. Maybe those involved simply couldn't wait to get back to their homes or their hotel rooms or maybe they had people waiting at those places who wouldn't look kindly on them bringing another person home for the purpose of sexual congress. So this woebegone stairway had to suffice. In his time, Castle had opened one door or another, top or bottom, and come upon such activity, and you'd be surprised the things people do and who they do them to, or with. Or maybe you wouldn't be surprised. The joint was open all day, all night.

The fourteen wooden stairs didn't prepare you for what was on the other side of the door they lead to. Inside it was all discreet lighting, banquette booths, polished ebony bar and 'Manhattan Club' in burnished aluminum above hundreds of crystal glasses hung upside down like glittering stalagtites.

"Whatta you know, whatta you say?"

The bartender and owner, Art Sprague, got bigger and bigger each year and he was big to begin with. A few months ago, Art had begun to curl the tips of his moustaches and now, come to think of it, reminded Castle of old pictures of John L. Sullivan. He was the only man Castle had ever seen who could wear a bowtie without looking silly.

"I know there's a fellow over to the library has a certain way with a bowtie, Art. Looks like competition to me."

"The hell you say. I ought to take myself over there and have a look. Would I be able to get in?"

"What? Get in the library? Sure they let all sorts of people in there."

"Usual?"

"Yeah."

Art never forgot a face or what kind of drink the person raised to his face. He might have had a career as a politician or a doorman at a hotel. But he was doing fine where he was. As long as he paid off the patch who came by every Friday for his envelope. In this town, the drinking of wine and spirits by men and women together in the same room was not only frowned upon, it was considered downright sinful—or so they said, the powers-that-be, the pillars of the moral community. They didn't frown upon the war though or sending the same men and women who weren't allowed to drink wine and spirits together over to foreign countries to fight or wrap wounds or drive ambulances and die.

Art Sprague set Castle's drink down before him with graceful motions of his big smooth hands. Napkin, glass, burnished metal bowl of pretzels. Said, "You working?"

"Yeah, sort of."

"Sort of."

"That's right. You know a guy named Myerhoff? Sells insurance. Maybe late Forties. Left his momma couple of years ago to live in the tenderloin?"

"He's a Presbyterian, comes in three times a week. Not the happiest guy in town but he's never any trouble."

Art Sprague didn't identify people by their religion but their drinks. Castle, for instance, was a vodka neat; at least in the Manhattan Club. Beanie Brown was a Boilermaker. Like that. So Rodney Myerhoff was a Presbyterian which is a rye and ginger.

"Heard he works in insurance," Castle said.

"Some white collar job. After work, he makes the rounds. Stops at Skinny's new place once a week."

"I heard Skinny's got a nice arrangement."

"Yeah, pays off the same people we all pay off. I was over there one time. Strictly business. I mean, not that kind of business."

"You mean not sexual congress business?"

"What I mean. So, Skinny, I hadn't seen her in four years. Well the dame has put on more weight than me even. This is one large woman."

"She was one large woman before. Came up to my office back in '36, had to take the freight elevator down. No lie."

"Need a crane now. But the thing is, she's, I don't understand it, she's still what they call curvaceous."

"She's no spring chicken either."

"They don't make dames like that anymore."

Castle had to agree.

"You seen Beanie around?"

"Last time, three days ago. He was in with a lime rickey and pair of draughts. Louis-Godoy coming up, I 'spect he'll be in doing business."

"I got to go do business. See you later, Art."

"Adios. Say hello to you-know-who for me."

"Come on, Art. Say her name. I want to see if you can do it without blushing."

Art couldn't hold Castle's gaze. Couldn't say the name 'Louise' either though he still blushed. He took up the rag, made like the ebony bar was in serious need of a vigorous buffing.

Castle called the Standard Building a few minutes before five and Laura told him he'd had two phone calls from somebody who wouldn't leave a name or a message, and one from Louise who said she had a rehearsal for the troop show later that evening and would meet him at the hotel.

Castle shrugged and sighed and tried to make like a melancholy lover, and when he was done the act, took himself to the Neon Angel on Abbott Street to meet Henry 'the Hipster' Heinz.

You knew you had to be at the right place because of the fantastic sign, over the door. A female angel, her neon blue wings flapping gently, a thing of beauty on a dreary street, waving disreputable customers inside, waving them good-bye.

You walked down three steps to a dank, narrow room thick with cigarette smoke, tables on each side of the wall leading to a small bandstand at the back and adjacent to a service bar. Even at a few minutes after five on a Tuesday evening the place was jumping, which on the surface might be explained by the factories and shipyards working three shifts. But once your eyes adjusted to the gloom, you had to wonder if this really explained the patrons, a good many of whom were junkies, hipsters, poufs and jaspers; of course, junkies, hipsters, poufs and jaspers might work in factories and shipyards but not these particular ones.

As Castle was summing up the place in a sociological sense, he heard his name called in the unmistakable high-pitched voice of Henry 'the Hipster'. "Hey, Gene. Daddy-o. Over here."

Henry was at the third table along the righthand side of the wall, seated with two other guys, and the three of them looked like contestants in a Bunny Berrigan lookalike contest. When Castle told them hello, one said "Aw reet" and the other, "Solid."

"So, man," said Henry, leaning close and saying, just north of a whisper, "Cat that copped my axe, my lovely C-Melody Sax is right over there at the band table. First table by the stage. Big Guy. You dig him there?"

"Red-haired, curly-haired gent nuzzling the blond."

"That's him."

"He just took your axe?"

"Other night, man. Like I told you when I fell out in the street."

"You ask him for it back? Ask him politely?"

"And impolitely too. Says I'm mistaken and it's not my axe."

"Could he be correct?"

"Nix, daddy. First, I know my own axe; second, the guy, man, he's a clarinet player. Can't even play that, let alone my C-Melody. The man is so square he has to walk around the block to turn over in bed. And he shows up at the Angel trying to play a C-Melody sax? Coincidence? Not likely.

"Yeah," agreed one of the Bunnys, neither of whom had spoken since 'all reet' and 'solid.'

"And if that ain't enough, I scratched three 'H's on the bell, down at the rim."

"Scratch another one," said the talkative Bunny, "and you

can bring a cow to the Pacific National Exhibition."

"So what do you want me to do, Henry?"

"I want you to get my horn, I'm supposed to work tonight at Skinny's new joint. She's been open two weeks, been promising music, and I got hired. Like I said, I'm not using no more."

"Too bad," said Bunny-two.

"Just a muggle now and again to relax me."

"So I go up to him, ask him for your axe and what am I supposed to do if he doesn't hand it over? Wreck the place?"

"If that's what it takes."

"You haven't mentioned moo-la."

"Well it just so happens that I'm holding," Henry said, and reached into the inside pocket of his too-tight suit jacket, brought out some bills, laid them out on the table, the Bunnys eyeing them avariciously.

"Well, that's different," Castle said, scooping up the two tens with only a slight thought for where the Hipster might have scored the money.

"For a double sawbuck you ought to have no qualms about wrecking the joint."

Castle got up, walked to the back of the place. There were four men and the blonde at the band table. The little saxophone lay across a chair next to the redhead. The blonde and the redhead looked at Castle when he got close but, to them, he would have been just another guy going to the bar. He did go to the bar. There was a woman who looked like Marie Dressler's tougher, older sister pulling beer and Castle got one from her. He drained half of it, turned away from the bar, said, "Gee, that's a fine looking C-Melody saxophone."

He took a step closer to the table.

"Yeah?" The redhead said.

"Oh, yes indeed," Castle replied. "Reminds me of one a pal of mine used to have. Why, heavens to betsy, I'd be willing to bet it is the very same one. I can see his initials scratched into the bell."

"Beat it, buddy. You know what's good for you."

"Sure I'll beat it, soon's you hand over the horn, let me return it to its rightful owner."

The red-haired guy, pushed back his chair and while he was in the process of standing up, Castle grabbed the horn with his right hand. The guy told Castle to let go of the fucking horn and Castle shook his head to indicate he wouldn't do that. The guy reared back his right hand, reared it back so far Castle had time to be reminded of a pitcher winding up with no runners on base, then to step in and throw a left hook over the guy's roundhouse, and it dropped the once-and-future clarinet player onto his keister.

The man looked up at Castle, all befuddled like he couldn't believe his favourite punch had let him down. Then he glanced at the blonde and must have figured he'd let her down too because he struggled to his feet and told Castle he'd get him now. But he didn't because Castle, the sax still in his right hand, jabbed him in the belly and jabbed him on point of the chin, and let go of that left hook again, and the guy went backwards over the edge of the bandstand and toppled into the drum kit. There was a hellatious racket that caused a hipster at the table to holler, "Big Noise From Winetka!"

Castle carried the little sax back to the Hipster's table, said, "Let's get out of here, go over to Skinny's."

Castle watched as the blonde turned her chair so her back was to the fallen musician who was hollering about being sucker-punched. Henry took the axe away from Castle and caressed it like a lover's face. He sent a few curses back to the redhead and they got out of there.

CHAPTER FIVE

"Come on in. If you know me you know how long it would take for me to get up and answer the door," was how Skinny O'Day answered Castle's rapraprap on her office door.

When he opened and she saw him, Skinny O'Day's exaggerated cupid's bow of a mouth widened to reveal tiny perfect teeth white as Chiclets.

"For you, Gene, I'll get up!"

She leaned forward, pressed two hands worth of sausage-like fingers, each of ten sporting a showoff ring, down on the top of her desk, grunted and heaved herself to standing, and Castle took in the sight.

Skinny O'Day had always reminded Castle of an arrangement of balloons. She must be three hundred pounds and sixty-five years old but Skinny still had it, though her chin now reminded him of a puffer fish and her bosom thrust forward like a balcony over the street.

"Yeah, I see you gawking at my rack, Gene. They ought to be a national monument. More men have clambered over them than Mount Robson. That's why my feet are so small, they never get any sun, rain neither. How's it hanging, partner? Though when you get a load of Skinny, it ought not be hanging!"

She took a step and he took a step and they embraced as much as possible. Castle's hands barely extended to her shoulders.

"You're a sight for sore eyes, Skinny."

"Admit it, I'm so outrageous, I could put lead in a dead man's pencil. Take a good look, Gene."

Skinny gave him a side view and a rear view. From the back she looked like Jean Harlow had been inflated with everything in scale.

"That's prime meat, boy. Back when we were with Northern Lights Attractions, you could have had me any time you wanted. But you missed your chance. I've made millions with this rear end and what I got down there, not to mention all the rest of it. My stuff is still satin and smooth. I've only had to do it once or twice a year, these last few years, and I still make more on that alone than our prime minister does or twice as much as this mayor we got with the name that sounds Italian but he's really a Scotsman. The prick what shut me down for a time. But the know-it-all went to Ottawa with his idea for an idiot highway to Alaska, of all things, and the boys in Victoria felt snubbed so they're putting him in his place and he's on the way out which is how come I've been able to reopen in these fine surroundings."

Skinny made a gesture with her right arm like she was throwing bread crumbs to pigeons. She was indicating the one-way window that afforded her a view of her operation.

"It is a swell looking joint, Skinny."

"Yeah, I can sit at my desk watching the goings on whilst nibbling fig newtons, unseen."

They both stared at the operation on the other side of the window. At the right of the picture, a quartet was playing although nothing could be heard in Skinny's office. To the left was a small bar, maybe fifteen feet long, four men standing there. In between was a small parlour. Two women sat on divans and Morris chairs being observed by men on other chairs. Another woman was at a table talking to a man. A fourth woman came walking down a staircase. No sooner did she reach the bottom, than one of the men got up from his chair and approached her. She smiled and retraced her route, him following close behind.

It was curious watching them without hearing anything. It was like being in a movie theatre watching the show with the sound turned off, sort of like it was before there was any sound to turn off. Christ, silents seemed like ancient history. And what was the distinguished old party—he had that silver-haired supreme court judge look to him—about to say to the young woman at the table? She was leaning forward, breasts about to spill out of her satin nightgown, all big-eyed and rapt attention as if she hadn't heard it all before.

"So, Skinny. You got the tall, raven-haired beauty that just disappeared upstairs and the three equally lovely dames I can see before me. Anyone up in the rooms?"

Skinny's wry smile vanished, the bow of her mouth drawn down at the corners.

"Nobody else up there except the dwarf—you know him— I hired him after Garmano's joint was kaput. And I don't rent him out. Though there's another operation in town, where a fellow or gal could rent something just like him."

"You're kidding me?"

"I'd kid about something like that? I don't know where it is. Don't want to know. But I do know you don't go there, survey the merchandise. You phone in your order. 'Hello, I'm in the mood for a legless Negro. Yes, you heard me right, a female legless Negro.' — 'You do? Well fine, then. When shall I come by?' That sort of thing. Only it gets weirder than that. Me, I run a respectable place with high-class girls. A little strange is all right, too strange and you're out the door, Jack. So, yeah, I got four girls. I had five. Which is why I left a message for you to come by. It is easier than me paying you a call. Remember the last time? That was humiliating."

"So tell me about the girl?"

"Sanora. You seen those paintings by those English people from the last century? Roselli. Rosinante, something like that?"

"Rosetti?"

"Yeah. All those wavy hair nymphs bathing in pools in sylvan glades. White, white skin and freckles like they were distributed from an angel's wand?"

"This girl look like that?"

"Almost. Only the only difference being that the nymphs in the painting don't look filthy-minded. This Sanora looks like a goddess on the skids and glad to be there. At first glance you get the idea she's too innocent for this veil of tears, needs somebody big and strong to take care of her. On second glance, she looks like she wants somebody big and strong to take care of her, all right, but in a different sort of way. She drove the men wild, I can tell you. I had to raise the tariff so she wouldn't get overworked. She went at five times—I mean it, five times—the going rate."

"Sounds too good to lose."

"She is. I can't afford to be without my star attraction. What with all the action in town. High rollers. War contracts. Get her back for me, Gene, whatever it costs, and don't spare the expenses. There's even a bonus in it for you, you know what I mean."

"I'll get right on it."

"No." The bee sting was back in place, the bemused smirk was back on Skinny's face. "You can get right on it after you find her."

"I'm on my way, Skinny. Just one thing. You know a guy called Myerhoff comes in here?"

"Sure."

"You know where can I find him?"

"Sure. When you leave my office, walk to the far end of the bar. He's the one in the blue suit, hair mussed. The one who's two drinks from his limit."

"What kind of guy is he?"

"Not the life of the party, not its pooper either. He likes his libations, likes his women, but he's never any trouble."

Castle told Skinny goodbye and put himself on the other side of the one-way window, walked across the room and sat at the end of the bar. Leaned against it, next to Myerhoff slumped on his stool, staring into his rye and ginger.

"Presbyterian," Castle said and Myerhoff, looked up, said, "What?"

"What you're drinking. Rye and ginger."

Myerhoff grunted. "Sounds like that could be a question that might stump Mister Smartypants. You should send it in."

"Maybe I will. How I recognized you. Somebody told me that's what you drink."

"Glad I'm popular. Why are you interested?"

"Your wife."

"I don't have one."

"Your former wife."

"Why? You want her for yourself? You have my blessings."

"No, I don't want her for myself. She hired me."

"For what?"

Castle told him the story. Myerhoff shook his head and looked sad, truly sad.

"When Billy died it was like something in her died too. A big something. She disappeared into her own mind. It was like living with one of those robots, only a robot that the scientists didn't put together correctly. I couldn't live with a robot anymore."

"Why would she hire me? Throw away that money?"

"She has nothing else to do. I feel sorry for her. But sorry doesn't do any good. I got my own life."

"You knew a girl used to work here named Sanora?"

"Is that any of your business?" There was no hostility in Myerhoff's voice. He just asked the question.

"Tell you the truth, it is my business on account of Skinny hired me to find her."

"You a cop?"

"I help people when they can't go the usual route. I find people mostly."

"I hope you find her. Sanora, well, she's not like anyone else. There're other women and then there's her. I mean when it comes to, well, you know."

"Yeah, I think I know what you're talking about."

"Sanora, she makes a guy feel like he's the best guy ever climbed into the sack with her or with any other dame. Yet, at the same time, you get the feeling that way down deep she's laughing at you. Not that she's obvious about it, more like she has no respect for you because she's watching you being over-whelmed by her. Thing is, you don't care. You know what I'm trying to tell you?"

"I think so."

"I hope you find her. I can't afford her anymore but I'd sure like to look at her, watch her walk around the parlour over there."

"See you around, Rodney."

Castle started for the door while the quartet was in the mid-dle of "Body and Soul," but he stopped to hear Henry the Hipster's solo; Henry copying Coleman Hawkins note for note, it sounding sweeter on the C-Melody. The guy could play.

Outside, on Homer Street, it was dark and fog had rolled in from the sea to hide the stars and make a guy turn up his collar. Castle didn't turn up his own collar but knew the fog could make you do that because of the fellow standing on the corner of Helmcken, just outside the circle of light made by the street lamp that was a few steps away. The collar belonged to a trenchcoat, and the man also had on a wide-brimmed hat that was called a slouch hat, sort of a big brother to a fedora. He fished a pack of cigarettes from his trenchcoat pocket, shook one out, stuck it in his mouth and began patting himself down. When I get a little closer, Castle told himself, he's going to ask me for a light.

"Say, pal. You got a light?"

The guy took a couple of steps and seemed like he was about to lean forward, dip his head and poke the cigarette in between Castle's cupped hands. Over the man's shoulder, on the wall of the corner store was a poster that showed a soldier with his finger up to his lips, "Shhh!"

"Sorry, I don't."

"You don't smoke?"

The man had the trace of an accent that Castle tried to place. Finnish maybe, Swedish or Norwegian.

"Cigar now and again."

"Good for you, it is a bad habit."

Castle nodded, told the man that it sure is, and was taking a step away, when the man said, "We have a friend in common."

"We do, eh?"

"Yes, we do. His name is Leandro."

"Leandro?"

"Yes."

"That's an unusual name. What is it? Italian?"

"It is hard to tell where our Leandro is from. Mallorca, perhaps; Guatemala, I don't know; he's never said."

"Oh."

"Leandro Martine."

"You a cop?"

"Not in this lifetime. I met Leandro in Spain, same place you met him. I wore the mono there."

"What colour was it?"

The man grinned. The mono was an overall worn by anarchist fighters during the Spanish Civil War.

"Blue. Look, I understand your need to be cautious. Leandro is in trouble. Serious trouble. Of course, he'd be in trouble if only because of the work he's doing but..."

"What's he doing? This Leandro fellow?"

"He's coordinating Resistance movements. There are still

some people in France, in Poland, Belgium, my own country, Norway, who are willing to fight. He is the link between us all."

"Admirable."

"Indeed. There are some willing to fight but there are more people willing to kill anyone involved in resistance and the one they want to kill the most is Leandro Martine. If this is not bad enough, his daughter has disappeared."

"His daughter! I didn't know he had a daughter."

"You did not know that this man you have never heard of had a daughter? Well, he does or he did."

"Where is he?"

"He is in Vancouver."

"Why hasn't he come to me for help?"

"In Europe, he can hardly stick his nose out of hiding without the most diligent planning. There he must go about in disguise with bodyguards also in disguise, who pretend to have nothing to do with him."

"Tell him to come to see me in disguise."

"You know better than that. He cannot do that here. Our enemies would know that if he is in Vancouver, he would try to contact you. They want to draw him out. That's why they took his daughter."

"But, wait…"

"Yes, I know. You have many questions. I will take you to him. But not now. Is tomorrow possible?"

"Yes. What do I do?"

"Someone will come to see you at your office at ten o'clock."

The man nodded his head and walked away. Castle watched him walk around the corner, and down Helmcken Street. When he was out of sight, Castle caught another glimpse of the soldier on the sign warning him to button his lip. In back of the soldier other soldiers were firing guns and a blast of flame was shooting out of the gun on a tank. "Don't worry about me," he told the soldier on the sign. "But you, you better duck down, private. If you know what's good for you."

Castle got back to the Rose Hotel and the room was cozy and familiar. Louise's dress and slip, thrown over the back of a chair, bra and panties on the seat, stockings across the bed. The bathroom door was open, he heard the water running. Louise called out hello. Castle took off his hat sailed it across the room, it landing perfect on the clothes hook on the wall near the window. From this angle he could make out the pink neon glow of the 'R.'

The bathroom door flung open and Louise stepped out, flung her arms wide, "Ta da…!"

She was wearing a military uniform—a woman's military uniform—of some sort, only it was tailored to accent every curve, the skirt hemmed shorter than any military skirt had a right to be.

"What do you think?"

"I think you go marching around the parade ground in that outfit, you'll be invaded. I didn't think the Wacs or the Waves or whatever you're supposed to be were allowed to have their garters showing."

"I'm a WREN, silly. And you said the line almost perfectly."

"What line?"

"Guy in the skit, says: Are you a Wac or a Wave, or what?' And I say, 'No, silly. I'm a WREN'…beat…'with a yen' …beat…'for men.' Then all the soldiers are supposed to go crazy."

"That doesn't sound like Eugene O'Neill."

"Oh, but it is. I assure you. And I do have a yen. For one man, anyway."

"Well your uniform does give me ideas."

"Then I'll leave it on. Get over here and do your bit for the military."

The next morning, nine forty-five, Castle was in his office, in his banker's chair, back to the door, feet on the windowsill, watching the rain fall in the shaft between buildings. He had an absolutely divine view of the adjacent window and, had he the notion, Castle could have opened his window, reached out and, by leaning forward all the way, just barely, with the tip of the middle finger of his right hand—after, of course, setting down the snub-nosed .38 calibre revolver that he now held in that hand—touched the neighbouring ledge. He was severely tempted; what the hell, life is nothing if not a panoply of new experience. But he restrained himself. After all, it wouldn't look right if a Resistance contact should walk through his door and see him leaning out his window that way. How would he explain himself? Also, at least half the window ledge was encrusted with guano. Castle wondered why the pigeons always rested on that one side and never the other. Were they merely creatures of habit? Or was there something sinister involved, maybe they could smell some long ago pigeon-eating eagle who had perched on the other side. Who knows?

By moving his chair closer to the window and looking to his left, Castle could see between the edges of the two buildings, just as they were about to merge in the distance, a horizon of, well, today it was a horizon of nothing. Of gray nothing. On a clear day there would be the inlet, the mountains beyond. This morning, he would have to content himself with conjuring ships out there, ships from exotic ports and faraway places. He could imagine himself just arriving, ready to step ashore with his mind on, hell, women is what his mind would be on, or at least one of them in particular. Or, he'd be setting off for distant lands, for he still had the urge to ramble and to roam. There'd be novelty and excitement. Yeah, Castle told himself, and there'd be a good chance I'd get shot at and a better chance I'd land in jail. Such things have happened in the past.

There was a knock on the door. The chair scraped as, on reflex, Castle started to turn. He made a mental note to price one of those chairs on rollers. He gave the gun a firm squeeze to remind it there might be work to do. This may be some kind of setup. They, whoever they were, had determined he knew Leandro Martine and, knowing it, had to waste him.

He approached the door on an angle but the person on the other side wasn't worried about showing a shadow and presenting a target. The visitor was standing right in front of the frosted glass as if wanting to press a nose to it, make faces. It wasn't a very tall person either because the letters GENE CASTLE were spread across the person's shoulders. Still that meant someone Joe Frontenac's size, and Joe could be dangerous.

Castle stood to the left of the door, half turned away from it, reached out and grabbed hold of the knob with his left hand, took a deep breath, pointed the gun and pulled the door open.

"Oh, my heavens!"

Mrs. Nora Myerhoff, raised her black patent leather handbag to her chest as if it would stop a bullet. Castle dropped his gun hand. Almost took the Lord's name in vain, but thought better of it.

"You nearly scared me half to death, Mr. Castle."

"I'm sorry, Mrs. Myerhoff. There are some dangerous characters lurking about. But please come into my office and we will talk."

"Yes, that is why I've come today, Mr. Castle. To talk with you about Billy. But, before I forget."

She opened her handbag and brought out a folded piece of paper, a page from a nickel notebook.

"There was a man at the top of the stairs just a moment ago. Come to think of it, he could be said to have been lurking about."

Castle looked at the piece of paper that Mrs. Myerhoff held in front of her.

"But he looked like a respectable sort of person. Anyway, the man asked me if I was going to see you and I told him I was, even though I thought it rather nervy of him to ask my business.

And he told me to give this to you."

Castle led Mrs. Myerhoff around the lacquered screen and into his office. He helped her remove her raincoat, draped it on one of the visitors' chairs, and indicated she sit in the other one. While she was getting settled, he unfolded the piece of notebook paper.

"Like the Norwegian said, someone came to see you at ten. Next step: be on a bench in Victory Square at 10:30 A.M. We met there once before. Signed, an old friend."

"We met in Victory Square?" Castle thought he said it to himself but changed his mind when he heard Mrs. Myerhoff speaking.

"You did? What an unusual place for you and Billy to meet. Does he have a job in the area?"

"Huh? Oh, yes. Well, no. I did meet Billy. Yes, we met in Victory Square. But he doesn't work in the area."

"Did you ask him to please, please come and see me?"

"Yes, but, Billy, well, he has a very important job in the military. Undercover work. Very hush hush. He didn't tell me much about it. Couldn't tell me much about it. Loose lips, don't you know. He did say that he would drive by but, uh, this time you probably won't be aware of it. I mean, of him coming by. Everything he does has to be secretive. He desperately wants to stop in and see you but he has to go out of town in just a very short time."

Castle got it out in a rush and exhaled, sat back in his chair, somehow feeling exhausted by what he'd said, the act of saying it. What he couldn't understand was that he'd had every intention of expressing his sorrow over Billy's accident. Of telling her how he understood that by hiring him she was giving in to the comforting illusion that things were not the way they are.

"He always was an adventurous boy. A good boy. And now, after what you've told me, he must also be a hero."

"Oh, yes, ma'am. A hero that's what Billy is. Some fight in uniform on the battle field, others work behind the scenes and their role is often just as dangerous, and it is certainly just as valuable. Yes, Mrs. Myerhoff, Billy is one of democracy's warriors."

Castle was amazed at himself.

She had tears at the corners of her eyes. Jesus, Castle said to himself, it is contagious. He looked at the notebook paper open on his desk, thought of the bottle of rum, the bottle of rye on the radiator behind him.

"I can't thank you enough, Mr. Castle."

"Oh, well, don't thank me, Mrs. Myerhoff. Yes, and another thing, Billy doesn't want you to worry about him. Due to the nature of his activities, he can't be in contact."

"I understand."

Mrs. Myerhoff stood up. Castle helped her back on with her rain gear, and walked her to the door.

She opened it herself.

"You did well, Mr. Castle."

"I hope so, Mrs. Myerhoff."

"Perhaps next year, I will come to see you again for more information about Billy."

"Anytime, you wish."

Castle watched her walk down the hall toward the stairs, a lonely woman with thick legs.

CHAPTER SIX

Ten minutes later, Castle went down to the lobby. Laura was busy at her board. He stood for a minute by the revolving door, looking out at the rain, the Shanghai Alley sign across the street. Tried to picture Johnny, the old-time Wobbly and his wife May, going down the Alley with their red wagonload of junk. Might as well picture Billy-boy while you're at it, he told himself. Are they, all three, on the other side of the curtain? Is there another side? If there is, does everyone go to the same place? An old freedom fighter like Johnny, an old radical pamphleteer like dear sweet Rose Tremaine? It's easy to imagine them cutting up jackpots on Cloud Nine. But what about some bastard like Augie Garmano or Henry Clay Frick? Or the creep that put down the Winnipeg General Strike? Hilliard Lyle was the bastard's name. Later killed his wife and one of his kids before shooting himself. Hard to picture Rose and Johnny and May hobnobbing with the likes of them, clinking heavenly flagons of nectar and ambrosia, clusters of cherubs floating around the table.

Castle shook his head, trying to banish such notions. If it is between an afterlife and a whole heap of nothing, and I was a bookie like Beanie Brown, I'd lay heavy odds against heaven and hell. Of course, I could lay whatever odds I wanted and nobody'd be around to collect. One way or the other.

Castle pushed on one of the wings of the revolving door and went outside. Appropriate thoughts for a guy on his way to meet somebody on a park bench in the rain, all on account of somebody other people want to kill real badly.

Victory Square occupies half a block of grass that slopes from Pender Street down to Hastings. It is bisected by a walkway lined with benches. He had his choice of benches since no one else was foolish enough to sit on a bench in the rain. At the bottom of the park is a cenotaph dedicated to all the people who gave their lives in the other world war which everyone now seems to forget was fought so another one would never be necessary. Castle had been in that one, in those foxholes filled with mud and shit and rats and corpses. He'd fired blindly into the night. Maybe killed German boys he never saw. Killed a couple he did see. He'd heard boys trapped in the barbed wire, listened to them all night screaming, "Mummy, Mummy!" Remembered one night in particular, the kid calling for his mama, over and over. For hours, it went on. The kid less than a hundred yards away. And all the rest of us huddling down deeper and deeper into the mud and shit, trying to pretend we couldn't hear it. Then the corporal from Montreal, screaming, "I can't stand it anymore you bloody bastard!"

And he fired six times into the kid.

Castle had gotten through that war without so much as a scrape. Fifty thousand Canadians dead at Vimy Ridge in April, '17, and the worst that happened to him was a sprained ankle from going over the top with a foot numb from cold.

As for all those local sons who were not so lucky, Castle wondered did they know they were commemorated by a stone statue that hundreds of people walk by everyday without taking any notice of whatsoever? Or were they beyond any knowing?

God, there's that question again.

The man came up the walkway from the northeast corner of the park. Medium height. He had on a raincoat and a hat such as you don't see out west, not even in Victoria. A brown woolen thing, two shades of brown, and a narrow brim just itching to be turned down. It made Castle think of Englishmen walking the hedgerow with a dog, also pedigree, shotgun folded over the forearm. The man had on a pair of horn-rimmed glasses. English aristocrats don't wear glasses, don't need them. Breeding, you know.

The man sat down on Castle's right, nodded, studied his face. Castle studied back. The man shook his head. "Don't recognize me, eh?"

"Something familiar about you. But I don't know many people from Ottawa."

"How do you know I'm from Ottawa?"

"Hell, if you think I should recognize you, that means we know each other or have known each other. You should, therefore, know what I do for a living, if that's what you call it. Hence, you should evince no surprise at me knowing where you're from. But to tell the truth, it is more like a guess. Not a wild guess but a guess, nevertheless. That rhymes."

"Yes, you're a real Sherlock Holmes. But tell me how you deduced where I'm from?"

"The way you're dressed. You have to be from the East but not all the way east like Halifax or someplace. You don't appear exhausted as you would had you made such an epic journey. Somehow you don't have the cosmopolitan Montreal look, if I may beg your pardon. It has to be Ottawa or Toronto, and I get strong emanations of government."

"I should be very impressed. You got all the details but not the identity. Here, does this help?"

The man took off the hat. There was a hint of a part on the right side of his head through hair too curly to have been matted down by the hat.

"No?"

"No," Castle said.

The man removed his glasses.

"I'm getting close," Castle said.

"Picture my hair longer and uncombed. Me wearing rimless glasses just like Rose Tremaine."

"Were you politically naïve but full of righteous piss and vinegar?"

"Yes, I'm afraid that sounds like me."

"Well, then, you have to be my old friend—if that's the right word—Martin Finnegan."

They shook hands. Four years ago, Martin Finnegan, who at the time resembled Leon Trotsky's skinny younger brother, was secretary of the Workers' Union Alliance. Their strike fund went missing and Castle was contacted to recover the money. For a time, Finnegan was a suspect. When Castle returned from Spain, Finnegan was long gone. Castle and Louise had joked that he probably wound up a minor Party functional in Minsk.

"So, Finnegan, tell me. Have you ever been in Minsk?"

"Minsk? What're you talking about? Oh, you heard I went to the Soviet Union. Didn't go to Minsk. I was in Omsk."

"Minsk. Omsk. Pinsk. I always figured they'd be like Prince Rupert. The main drag there. Listen, just like Rupert, it's raining."

"I know."

"Let's go somewhere and talk. I assume you're the person I'm supposed to meet whilst sitting on a bench."

"That's me, Castle."

"And therein lies a tale. Which you can tell me somewhere that is safe. Unfortunately, the Manhattan Club, which is right across the street and down a ways isn't safe for this sort of thing. So we will repair to the Seaman's Club."

They walked out of the park and down to Hastings Street, and hailed a cab that had been going east. No sooner were the doors closed than the driver muscled the wheel all the way to the left and crossed four lanes of traffic to get them going west. He almost ran over a woman about to step out between two parked cars.

"Missed," the driver said. "Heh, heh."

"Yeah," Castle agreed. "You didn't run her over but you got her wet."

"She was wet anyway."

The woman had reminded him a bit of Nora Myerhoff.

"Hey!" the driver exclaimed. "You're the private eye character. I've given you a ride a few times over the years."

"Oh, yeah. I remember you. You're the guy…" Castle gave Finnegan a nudge with his elbow… "who never forgets a face."

Finnegan hunkered down, looked out the side window.

"That's me."

"What about my buddy here?"

"Looks familiar. I might have picked him up one time but he wasn't wearing a hat."

"Must have been somebody resembled him," Castle said. "My friend Steve here just got in town from Halifax. First time on the coast."

"Nah, no way. I've seen him before."

Castle met the driver's eyes in the rearview mirror.

"Yeah, well, listen, buddy," Castle said. "Given your fantastic memory maybe you can help me out."

The driver sat up eagerly, ready for an assignment.

"It is a dame I'm looking for."

"Me too."

"Funny guy. You better get your eyes out of the rearview mirror though because you just went through a red light."

"Yeah, yeah. What about the dame?"

"I've never seen her. But she's a working girl's been stolen. I'm told she manages to look innocent and degenerate at the same time."

"Her I want to find."

"She looks like she should be gliding through sylvan glades in a flimsy gown."

"With me chasing her. Can you picture it?"

"I don't want to. No offense, pal. But you in a flimsy gown?"

"With my cabby's cap. That's not much to go on, that description."

"Are you kidding? That's more of a clue than I usually get. Shouldn't be anything to it. An innocent, degenerate red head with freckles."

"I'll keep an eye out."

Castle found an old betting slip in his coat pocket, wrote his phone number on it for the cabby.

"Call me, you see any dame looks like that."

"I hope I get the reason to call you. I've had my share of unusual dames in here in the past year. Actually, most of them in the past month on account of how things've got real hot in Europe. What with all the activity, factories working triple shifts, women working in them, the services mobilizing, dames servicing the soldiers. Where were they all before? All these women? You kind of hate to think of husbands going off to war, the little lady shedding her apron and putting on her fancy threads to go downtown and jitterbug all night. I mean if I went to the club and jitterbugged with them, it wouldn't seem so wrong. But I think of them guys fighting for democracy while their dames are having a good time back home, well, I wouldn't think it was right."

"That's life, pal."

"And the fancy threads they put on. I mean, the war is sure good for women's fashions. These two bints got in the back, yesterday, eh? They work in North Van. Riveters or like that. Wear dungaree overalls to work, come home, turn into dames like you'd see pedalling their ass on the street in Paris, France. 'Darling!' gushes the one. 'I simply adore your shoes. Wherever did you get them?' Well I'd gotten a load of the bint's shoes when she stepped into my cab. They had heels on them most have been five inches high. 'What are they covered with?' asks the one. 'Linen' says the other one. '$8.95 at Ingledew's.' You would not, I guarantee you, you would not have seen any woman wasn't a professional wearing shoes like that before the

86

war. And these were two normal sort of women. You want un-normal? Huh?"

"Yeah, give me un-normal but make it snappy because we're only two blocks from the Seaman's Club."

"Yeah. Dame gets in the other night. Pick her up by the train station, Main and Terminal. She gets in. Real tall. How tall're you, bub?"

"Six feet tall."

"She's got several inches on you. Anyway, it is not raining, you remember. Warm night. She takes off her sweater as she gets in, and, holey moley, the dame's got muscles. Her shoulders, it's like she's got baseballs on the ends of her shoulders, arms like thick ropes, veins all down her forearms. Jesus, I almost have a dozen accidents cause I keep looking in the mirror at her."

"Yeah," Castle said. "Takes all kinds."

"Sure does. Here we are. Seaman's Club."

He pulled to the curb. Finnegan paid him. The guy told him thanks, said, "The dame?"

"Yeah?" said Castle.

"I couldn't resist getting nosey. I let her off, I say, 'Jesus, lady. How you get those muscles?' You know what she said?"

"No, I don't."

"She says, 'Jesus had nothing to do with it. It was barbells and Indian clubs.' How'd you like that?"

Castle shook his head, as if to say, 'Yeah, that's something.' Then told the guy he'd see him around.

Castle led Finnegan up the stairs to the Seaman's Club above Goody's Goods. Goody in his store coughing into his hand, taking money from a customer. The guy holding a peavey hook in his other hand.

Castle had to sign his guest in, and after saying a few hellos and how ya doins to the old salts, found them a table in a quiet corner. Finnegan who'd never known the place existed, looked around, taking everything in, especially the photographs of members who'd gone to Davey Jones' locker. That lead him to discourse on the radical involvement with the shipping trade which, in turn, gave Castle his lead to inquire about Finnegan's own politics.

"So the last we met, you were still a dedicated party member," Castle said, and Finnegan flinched involuntarily, looked around the room.

"Don't worry, no scissorbills in here."

"All right. I may have been an idealist but don't worry, I haven't gone over to the other side."

"You haven't? You work for the government, right?"

"You think I'm on some official government-approved mission to help the man because he's probably the most important left-wing radical in the world?"

"Left wing? The man's an anarchist."

"Yeah, well."

"I remember correctly, anarchists were anathema to a guy like you."

"I'm a realist."

"So would it be closer to the truth to say you are on an unofficial mission?"

"It would be. I don't have a title. Should you go to Ottawa, to the government buildings, you won't find an office with my name on the door. In fact, if you button-hole the Prime Minister, he'll play dumb."

"He's good at that. Maybe only his pooch knows you exist."

"Pat."

"He give you your instructions, Pat?"

"Perhaps indirectly. You know Mr. King communes with his dead mother?"

"I don't want to think about it. Let's get down to brass tacks, as they say."

"Right. Last year, you met Leandro Martine in Ramona's."

"How'd you know that?"

88

"Martine told me through an intermediary. But I would have found out eventually."

"Why Mr. Finnegan don't tell me you're a…"

"Don't say it. I told you I have no title. Let me just say that this is a situation, I mean the world situation, that makes for unlikely allies."

"Yeah, like Hitler and Stalin."

Finnegan sighed, nodded wearily. "Let me continue. The reason Martine is over here has to do with his daughter, Isabella, whose mother is English. After the debacle in Spain, Martine was, well, it doesn't matter exactly what he was doing. Suffice it to say that he was up to his old tricks. He refused to go into melancholy exile as did so many others involved with the Republic."

"What the hell is the guy anyway? His nationality."

Finnegan shrugged, "I thought you anarchists had no nationality."

"This guy's had plenty of them. Durutti's men in Spain used to talk about Leandro all the time. Pass parts of the legend around like they were playing cards. They couldn't agree on any-thing, especially not his background. They said he was an aristo-crat from Uruguay, the black sheep of one of the richest families of Guatemala, a Maltese fisherman's son, even Swiss."

"I honestly haven't a clue. I do know his wife is English, and comes from an aristocratic family hence the added impor-tance—in certain circles—of this mission that I'm going to tell you about."

"So, a mission it is?"

"Yes, it is. All of that. You will be well rewarded."

"Depends if I work for you or not."

"You will."

"You've become sure of yourself as the years go by, eh, Mr. Finnegan?"

"In this situation, I am sure of myself. And of you."

"Okay. Lay it out, Jack."

"Last year. Not even a year ago, actually. October. Martine arrived in Vancouver to check on possible temporary homes for his daughter. That's what he was about when you met him in Ramona's. When nothing happened, I mean, when nothing happened to Merry Old England, Martine's wife convinced him that it was not necessary to spirit the child overseas. There was also the stigma of The Children's Evacuation. That was highly criticized for being, in reality, a rich children's evacuation. His wife, his wife's family, didn't want any part of that. But not too long ago when Hitler upped the ante, the English began evacuating children of all classes. Of course, now that an invasion of the island is feared, ships crowded with kiddies are leaving Liverpool accompanied by warships. Anyway, Isabella, twelve years old and a beautiful girl judging by her photographs—fine English features but darker colouring, call it Spanish colouring—had to leave.

"As you know, Martine is a wanted man. Much wanted. Kalju—that's who you met yesterday—told you that Martine coordinates Resistance movements in all the occupied countries. He is, quite frankly, a hero. More than that, he is a symbol. There are many people who want him dead. Time and again, in Spain and a dozen other places, he has proven impossible to find much less to kill. Hell, who do his enemies look for, a South American or a Swiss?"

"Maybe a guy with darker colouring? Call it Spanish colouring?"

"He speaks," Finnegan letting that pass, "a dozen languages fluently and is a master of disguise."

"I regret to say that I believe I know where this is leading."

"Yes," Finnegan nodded. "The girl."

"Follow the little girl."

"They did. Whoever they are. Apparently, Isabella and her mother, Iris, have been watched closely and constantly since the war began. Unfortunately, our enemies had several of their people on board the evacuation boat, one acted as the girl's chaperone. After the boat docked in Montreal, the chaperone and two ladies from the Agency, legitimate employees, put Isabella on the train. The chaperone accompanied her all the way across the country. When the train reached Vancouver, the fake chaperone introduced the little girl to her Canadian guardians who, of course, were not the family with whom Martine had made arrangements."

"What happened to the real family?"

"The Eversons. A bright young couple. Their father had been an organizer in the mines."

"Ellis Everson," Castle said. "Yes, I met him a few times. That was a good lineage. His father before him battled Dunsmuir in the coal mines on the Island."

"Well the lineage came to a halt the morning of the day that Isabella Martine or, rather, Tree, arrived by train in Vancouver. It seems the Eversons had an unfortunate automobile accident in the Fraser Valley on their way to pick her up. Nevertheless, a couple using their identification did meet the little girl. And that is the last we know of her."

"You get a description of these people?"

"Unfortunately, no. We have to assume they would have been approximately the age of the Eversons."

"What about Leandro?"

"He got into town a couple of days ago. He is in hiding, of course. And in disguise. You can imagine that he is frantic. He wants to search for his daughter but he can't show himself. The people who have Isabella are waiting for him to do just that."

"Do you know where he is?"

"No, I don't. I know where his associate Kalju is. Or, at least, I know where I am supposed to take you to meet him. Assuming you want to embark upon this mission."

"Lead on Mr. Finnegan."

The guy behind the wheel of this taxi was not the chatty sort. He took them east on Georgia, over the Viaduct, south on Main and left on Terminal. Nobody had spoken a word until they were stopped at the traffic light across from the train station at Main Street. "Imagine what the little girl was feeling," Finnegan said. "Stepping out of the train after her long journey. Eight days by ship, five days across country. Leaving the station and coming out onto the street. Two strangers holding her hand."

Castle grunted, looked at the picture Finnegan had just painted then turned his attention to Finnegan himself. Surprised by his seeming concern for the little girl. The young man he used to know named Martin Finnegan wasn't interested in people, only in The People. He had been the kind of member who kept the Party alive. A single-minded idealist. Able to overlook all sorts of things, at least until the Hitler-Stalin pact. There was no End that justified that. Or could there be another reason for Finnegan's turn around?

They got off on Terminal Avenue, just before the bridge over the railway yards, and before a two-story redbrick building with six blacked-out windows on each floor like a dozen dead eyes. Sign over the entrance doors read: DEEP SLEEP MATTRESS. A smaller sign on the right hand door hinted that the office was somewhere on the other side. Finnegan walked right up the path like he was a big buyer from Ottawa eager to purchase an entire boxcar load of double mattresses for hardworking bureaucrats who were desperately in need of some deep sleep. But instead of marching through the door that led to the office, Finnegan made a snappy squad's left, and led Castle around to the back of the building where three trucks were backed up to three loading ramps. There was nobody around. Maybe all the workers deserted the place at lunch hour.

Castle watched Finnegan pay close attention to the radiators of the trucks. Then he looked at Castle and pointed to an 'x' chalked onto the middle radiator just below the cap. Finnegan bent down like a catcher in his crouch, and felt around the inside of the front bumper. He brought a piece of paper out from where it had rested on the lip of the bumper, took a look, crumpled it up and put it in his pocket. "He's down here," Finnegan said to Castle.

They walked to the far corner of the asphalt covered loading area and followed a path that lead down a hill to the train tracks. When they reached the bottom, Finnegan turned to his right and immediately stopped. There were half a dozen people standing by the side of a track, their heads bent.

"I know that stance," Castle said. "They're either having a prayer meeting or looking at something dead on the ground."

"See the switch out there," Finnegan indicated a railroad switch fifty yards out from where the six people were gathered. It was on the other side of three spur lines, on a sort of island between other tracks. "Kalju said to meet him along the path, and adjacent to the switch."

They walked closer, and Castle said, "I don't see the man who stopped me last night. This Kalju."

"No. These people look like train workers and hoboes. Except for the woman. Or maybe she's a yard clerk."

"Yeah, so I'm afraid I have a pretty good idea who that must be on the ground getting all the attention. The thing is, do you want to stick around, given your sensitive position?"

"Yes, there is that to consider. What about you?"

"I don't have a position to consider, let alone a reputation. Also, I think I know one of the bo's. I'll come up with an excuse if the bulls come by and I get yaffled."

"Get what?"

"Grabbed by the cops."

"Maybe you should speak English."

"Thanks for the advice. I feel more relaxed now that you're sounding like the Finnegan of old."

"Right," Finnegan said, nodding curtly. "I'll get going. Let me know what happens."

"How do I get in touch?"

"Easy. Stop by the Hotel Vancouver. Ask for Mr. Engels' room."

"Frederick?"

"Fred."

Finnegan started up the hill and Castle continued on to his rendezvous with a dead man.

CHAPTER SEVEN

The six people watched him approach. He recognized High-Line Mason right away in his John B. Stetson hat, and despite it being a good decade and a half since last seeing him and, although the old hobo had to now be well past sixty, he didn't seem to have aged at all. There was another bo on Mason's right, a wiry fellow maybe forty years old. Mason nodded at Castle and nudged his buddy. The railroad workers looked at him suspiciously. The young woman regarded him with a blank expression.

"What do you want?" said the younger of the workers. He was wearing striped overalls and cap, holding a lantern. Castle glanced at the dead man before replying. It was, as he expected, the man who had approached him the night before.

"Are you a cop dressed as a brakeman?" Castle finally replied.

"No, but…"

"Why don't you answer our question?" asked the other worker, who had on dungaree pants and a dungaree jacket.

"Am I on railroad property?" Castle asked his own question.

"No, but it's sort of suspicious, you appearing out of the blue."

"I didn't appear out of the blue. I appeared out of the green bushes on the hill and, since neither of you fellows are cops and I'm not on railroad property, your questions are impertinent."

"I think you have a smart mouth," said the guy with the lantern.

"You better get hep and watch your step," High-Line Mason addressed the man, raising a chubby finger in warning. "I've seen Gene tussle, he's got the muscle as well's the punch, and today, man, you won't be eating lunch. When you see him move, you'll be humbled, you'll be awed; he'll take the lamp, stick it in your mouth, then you'll really be lantern-jawed. It'll be breaking, your jaw, that's the price of not taking…my advice. So Mister brakeman, try and be nice."

The railway men were so dismayed, they seemed rather comical. They looked from the old hobo to Castle, and back. "Well what the fuck."

"I always have a rhyme. High-Line's my byline. I've roamed all over the nation and I got a poem for every occasion." Mason removed his cowboy hat and displayed the inside of it. "I take off my bonnet and you see it is filled with sonnets."

A variety of scraps of paper were stuck in the inside brim of his hat. Highline plucked one of these, unfolded it and cleared his throat.

"What the fuck," the tall railway man said again. "Let's get away from these nutcases."

"The cops'll be looking for you Bolsheviks," the brakeman said.

High-Line watched after the departing workers. He shook his head. Extended his hand. "Howdy, Gene. What I should of said was 'This here's Castle and you sure as hell don't wanna see him wrassle.'"

"You did fine, High-Line."

"Catching ain't it. This here's my friend Weyburn Willie,

but I don't know about the filly."

As Castle shook Willie's hand, the young woman said, "Oh, I work up at one of the factories there. I just came down for a walk on my lunch break. I better be getting back."

Castle nodded at her. Just out for a walk in the rain instead of hanging out in the employee's room. She was in her mid-twenties, short black hair under a blue and white bandana.

He turned his attention back to the dead man.

"What's this all about, High-Line? You know?"

"We were back there in the trees just shootin' the breeze then we heard some jangling or should I say wrangling."

"Come on, pardner. Speak to me in free verse."

"Willie and me, couple of the other boys were jungled up, keeping out of the rain, fire going to keep the chill off. Heard some noises that didn't sound like Mahatma Gandhi and his boys, so we came for a look-see. Ain't that right, Weyburn?"

"Way it was, High-Line."

"We hustled over and found this unfortunate hombre same as you see him now. Only the blood was still oozing from the wound on the side of his head whereas now it has stopped and is starting to clot or whatever you call it. Congeal, if you will. Whoops, sorry."

"No sign of anyone around?"

"Not even the rustle a mouse'd make," High-Line said. "You know this bird, Gene?"

Castle glanced at Weyburn Willie.

"Weyburn's good people, Gene."

"I met the man once and I was supposed to meet him twice. Only I got here too late."

Castle wanted to go through the dead man's pocket's but the railroad men were standing under the eaves of the brake-man's shack watching. It wouldn't do to have them singing to the cops.

"Don't make no sense standing here getting wetter than we already are," Willie said. "Let's wait in the jungle for the bulls."

High-Line nodded and Castle followed them down the path and through a copse of alder. Four men were sitting under an awning made from a canvas tarpaulin and tree branches, and suspended between trees. There was a table top on tree stumps, a pot on the table, steam rising from it. The men were eating from tin plates but looked up when High-Line and Willie came into camp with the newcomer. "This is Gene Castle, he'll be my friend 'til the end. He's ridden the rails and been in the jails. There's a fellow down the path with his head smashed in. He'll never get up again. The bulls're on their way and I don't have to tell you who they'll suspect first. So if any of you have any secrets besides the ordinary ones you best duck out the back door."

In addition to the jerry-rigged dining area, there was an old truck, a delivery van. The back doors were open and Castle saw bedding in there. There were a couple of shelters made out of scrap wood and sheets of tin. A very cozy little camp.

"No sense me making a run for it. I wouldn't get very far." This came from a man with white hair and a white beard long enough that he had it tucked between the third and fourth buttons of his plaid shirt. His thin face was all ridges and wrinkles, seams so deep you could have hidden dimes in there.

"Well, I can put some space between me and them," said the youngest of the men, a kid who didn't look like he'd been out of his teens for very long. The kid Castle had seen the other day at Ramona's, talking to Matty Muldoon. "I don't fancy another jolt."

The kid put down his plate and fork. Buttoned his jacket.

"See you fellas down the line."

And with that he ducked into the trees. They listened as the bush rustled. After a moment, High-Line, looking at Gene, said, "That was the Alberta Kid."

He jerked his thumb at the old man, "That there isn't Methuselah, just his younger sibling, Laramie Stribling."

"That ain't a moniker neither," the old man assured Castle with a smile, his eyes pale blue like robins' eggs in their nests.

"Real name. Born in Wyoming. My folks named all us kids after towns in the state. Had me a sister named Cheyenne. Prettiest thing. Indians got her. Took her away. Brought her back and left her on the porch. This was back in, oh, musta been '72. I musta been fifteen years old."

Laramie stopped talking and returned to eating. Castle noticed his big yellow teeth.

"Gene, steal over to the table, grab yourself some slumgullion. These other boys are Fry Pan Charlie, so named 'cause of his fame, his fabulous feats providing us bos with delictable eats."

Fry Pan smiled broadly but it seemed forced, maybe he was embarrassed.

"The other one there, we call Algiers. On account of he speaks English with a French accent and can be real suave and he puts me in mind of Charles what's his name of movie fame. Boy-yeah. And that movie from a couple of years back, *Algiers*."

This other man had long black hair and fine features. He stood, wiped his hands on his pants and offered one to Castle, "But, I am so pleased to meet you, monsieur."

"You too," Castle said, shaking his hand, wanting to say, Come off it already.

Castle was about to hunt up his own tin plate when he heard commotion on the other side of the trees and the unmistakable voice, like a foghorn in the basement, of Chief of Detectives Horace Koronicki.

"Murphy, head back up the hill. Call the coroner, tell him what we got."

The five men stood, waiting. Detective Bartoli was first through the trees. Very un-cop-like, he let the surprise show on his face when he saw Gene Castle. Koronicki was a few seconds behind him, and stepped, huffing and puffing into the clearing. Koronicki was looking at the ground, trying to catch his breath, Bartoli prodding him in the side with the back of his right hand.

"What?" Koronicki said, looking up. "What?"

The Chief looked where Bartoli pointed.

"So? It's Gene Castle surrounded by four tramps. One of them old enough to be Jesus' uncle. Castle's wearing a light-weight overcoat, the rest of them dressed like, well, tramps. Maybe he's here giving them fashion tips."

"Listen, Gramps. We're neither bums nor tramps. We're hoboes for your edification, part of a long tradition. We're different, you see. You want to know anymore just ask me."

Koronicki just stared at High-Line Mason. Castle expected him to tear a strip of the bo's hide but all he did was shake his head and say, "Jesus goddamn Christ."

When he didn't add anything else, Danny Bartoli looked at him. "Boss?"

"Maybe I'm getting too old for this job," Koronicki said.

The Chief suddenly did look old—not old and spry like Laramie Stribling—just old and tired. Castle felt a brief, very brief tug of sympathy for him.

"Or maybe it's the world that's changing. Getting too complicated for me. Ever since the goddamned war started. It has been crazy." Koronicki shook his head. "We've had young kids killing each other over narcotics, Negro women sticking high heel shoes in the heads of Negro men. What happened to simple old fashioned murders? People are crazier too. Why just the other day, I heard about some place where you can phone in your weird sexual kink and they'll provide it within twenty-four hours."

"I heard about that too," Castle said.

"Shut up, Gene. I mean, Castle."

"And now I get to meet a bum—Oh, I'm sorry, sir. A HOBO—who don't talk like everyone else in the world, he spouts poetry."

"It is true I poeticize but High-Line Mason never lies. If I may be so bold, it's true you must be getting old. Sure the world she's achanging but High-Line's always been ranging. From shore to shore and more. When you, sir, were a mere lad I visited Baghdad. Of course, I was on the lam but in the bazaar I recited Omar Khaiyam."

Castle looked at the poet with admiration.

"I didn't think you were going to pull that off at the end."

"Me neither."

"Enough of the poetry circle. We got a dead body. What do you birds know, what do you say?"

Weyburn Willie told them that they'd heard scuffling, and that he and High-Line went to investigate. The other three—he, of course, didn't mention the Kid—stayed put. The man was dead when they got there.

"And Castle," Koronicki said. "It is to be expected that with a dead body present, you are on the scene. But why, exactly, are you here? Last dead body we found, a couple of days ago, you may recall, it, or he, had your name on a piece of paper in his pocket. The note wasn't so easy to read on account of blood got on it from the place where somebody put a knife into his chest."

"Professor Treherne," Castle said.

"Oh, no," High-Line muttered. "Why, he…" High-Line didn't finish the sentence.

"Why he, what?" Koronicki demanded. "You knew the man?"

"Everybody knew the Professor. He was a friend to the working man and those in distress. This is a matter that must be redressed."

High-Line spoke it sadly.

Castle had been watching High-Line and over his shoulder caught a glimpse of the man called Algiers. The hobo looked him in the eye, dipped his chin ever so slightly then looked away.

"The Chief asked you a question, Castle."

"I know he did Bartoli. And I'll answer it. I heard that my old friend High-Line Mason was down here and I came to see him. We go way back. High-Line was a friend of my father, and a friend to me after my father died."

"And you just happened to run into a dead body when you

run into the hobo, and he knows all these other radicals."

"Listen, Danny."

"Don't call me that."

"Listen, Danny. You ought not to worry so much about these wandering workers as about the good solid homegrown fascists who want to put people with complexions like yours and last names like Bartoli in camps for aliens. The country you were born in is at war with the country you are in."

Bartoli spoke angrily in Italian. And Castle spoke back to him in Italian. Bartoli was surprised to hear the words come out of Castle, but not as surprised as Koronicki was. "What did you say to him, Castle?"

"I told him he would need help if he tried."

"When did you learn to talk Italian?"

Castle addressed himself to Bartoli, "Don't you hate it when they say it like that, 'Eye-tal yun'?"

Bartoli kept the hard eye on him. Angry at being ranked in front of his Chief.

"I learned it in Abssynia," Castle said to Koronicki, looking at Bartoli. "That was a country independent for a few thousand years until the Italians invaded it, under one of Mussolini's generals, name of Graziano, a guy who didn't wear lifts in his shoes like Il Duce. You know, Mussolini, the pint-sized fascist mameluke with the bald dome."

"He's a visionary, Mussolini," Bartoli said. "He's done a lot of good for Italy."

"Not for the architecture," Castle said. "He is a visionary though. He could see what Hitler wanted to do to him so he didn't waste any time, just handed him the vaselina and bent over." Bartoli made a move but Koronicki stepped in front of him.

"Don't let him rile you, Danny," Koronicki said, and turned to Castle. "We ought to take you in."

"What for? Insulting the enemy?"

"We ought to take the lot of you in. And we would too. The two guys working in the yards want us to take you in but then another train worker came out of the cute little shed they got there and said the dead man was talking to somebody even taller who was wearing a long coat came down to the ankles. Now the dead man looks to be about six-foot-two inches tall or I should say six-foot-two inches long on account of he'll never stand up again. The other one was half a foot taller than him even, which translates to somebody taller than any of you birds. Now, one of you could have been wearing lifts in your shoes but—."

"Maybe it was Mussolini did it," Castle said, giving Bartoli a sidelong glance. "He wears lifts in his shoes."

"Don't push me, Castle."

"Naw. Wasn't Mussolini," Koronicki shook his head. "On account of he's bald and the other person had short black hair combed forward. None of you has short black hair. The French-looking fellow there has long black hair, it might have grown out real fast in an hour but same time as his hair was growing longer, he would have been growing shorter. So, I guess I can't haul any of you in as much as I'd like to."

"Well, then I guess there's nothing much left for you to do, is there, Chief Koronicki?

"Why, Mr. Castle, I could think of some things to do. Search the little boyscout camp, for instance."

"Maybe you'll find some muggles."

"Shake these fellows down for their identification."

"Might as well, nothing else to do, Chief. Two dead bodies in three days. Lots of war racketeering going on. Sure, search old Laramie there. Maybe you'll find some love letters from Annie Oakley."

"Hah!" chortled Laramie Stribling, slapping his knee. "That's a good one, that is. Why I only met Annie once but what everybody knew was that she didn't write love letters to fellows just to gals."

"You mean," said Castle, "she went that way?"

"Yes, indeedy."

Koronicki made a face like he took it as a personal affront, being in the presence of the type of people, one of whom, any-way, would have anything to do with someone of the jasper persuasion.

"We're going to keep on eye on you people," Bartoli said.

Koronicki grabbed him by the elbow.

"Let's go."

And he and Bartoli went.

When they were out of sight and hearing, Castle spoke first, "You got any of that stew left?"

"Sure enough," Weyburn Willie said. "Get you a plate and fork out of the truck. There's a clean tin cup on the nail there."

Castle fetched his slumgullion and sat at the table under the canvas tarp. High-Line asked about the Professor, and Castle told him how Treherne had been stabbed to death on Hastings Street. High-Line said that the Professor had been jungled up in the camp until a couple of days ago. But a hobo not coming back to camp was nothing to remark upon. High-Line didn't say any-more about the matter, a fact that was not lost on Castle.

The men took to cutting up jackpots. Or, at least, High-Line Mason and Laramie Stribling told stories. The other three most-ly listened. Laramie asked High-Line if he'd ever run into a par-ticularly nasty yard bull down in Youngstown, Ohio.

"'Deed I did. You mean Big Mean Sid. He's been known to take the cudgels to man, woman or kid."

Fry Pan, Weyburn knew of him too. Algiers said he hadn't travelled much in that part of the U.S. of A. The two old-timers traded tales about the notorious train cop, tried to come to an agreement on how many hoboes he'd killed in his day. They fig-ured it had to be somewhere between twenty-five and thirty.

"If I could be granted my very last wish," said High Line, "it'd be to go to Ohio and knee cap that son-of-a-bitch."

"Well, sir," Laramie said with a smile. "You'd have to dig him up out of the ground to do that."

"What! Well, I'll be damned. I hope he didn't pass pleasantly."

"No, Big Mean Sid got beat to death."

"I hope it was a 'bo what done it."

"No, sir. Weren't no 'bo. It were his wife. Way I hear it, Sid hadn't whupped any hobos, tramps, bums, old women or little children for at least three days and he must have been all tensed up on account of it. Gets home and decides to take it out on the little woman, who wasn't little enough. She took hold of the big, cast iron skillet that was on the stove full of hot lard for making Sid's favourite dumplings, and just made one of them decisions, you know, like 'I've had enough of this crap,' and she threw the grease in his face. Sid's ascreaming and athreatening, and Mary Lou—that's her name—she done lifted the skillet up over her head and brought it down on Sid's head, and he hit the kitchen floor bellowing, pleading for mercy like he never gave woman, child or 'bo. I guess Mary Lou figured since he was on the floor anyway, there was no sense him ever getting up or there'd be hell to pay, so she swung down on him three or four more times. And that was it for Big Mean Sid."

"That," said High-Line. "Calls for a drink."

After a couple of drinks and a few more stories, Castle got up to leave. The others shook his hand and the guy they called Algiers announced that he needed to stretch his legs, and walked out of camp with him. The man didn't speak until they reached the trail, and that wasn't until Castle remarked upon the weather, how you could always count on rain in June. Just when May had you thinking, despite yourself, that seven months of the stuff had finally ended, and now... Algiers interrupted, saying, "I'd say my disguise works rather well."

The man stopped on the path as if allowing Castle to study him.

"You had me fooled. I took you for what you were supposed to be, a hobo from back east, Quebec or New Brunswick, maybe. But don't be too proud of yourself because I've only seen you that one time."

"Yes, and how is your lady friend? Your accomplice, so to speak?"

"Louise. She's fine. Do any of those bos know about you?"

"No. It is a good cover."

"Look, Finnegan told me all about your situation. I want to help you but I don't know how to begin to do that."

Leandro Martine looked away, over at the train tracks, the factories silhouetted against a leaden sky. He had lived in many countries, under various names, had commanded armies, had honours heaped upon him, and now he looked like what he was pretending to be: a man wandering alone. Yes, the disguise works great, Castle thought, and the desperation on his face is a stroke of genius.

"Kalju was a good man. An old friend. We met in Norway before the Germans arrived and we had to flee. We worked together in France also. Now, he is gone. And the kind old man, Professor Treherne. It is I who asked him to find you. This was just before Kalju arrived. Perhaps, this Martin Finnegan can send someone to me. Gene, you do not have children, do you? May I call you Gene?"

"Yes, you may. And, yes, I do not have children."

"Then you cannot know what it is like to have your child stolen. I am going crazy with worry and with frustration at not being able to do anything."

"I know a guy I'll send down here. You saw him that time in Ramona's. He can be the go-between. I'll help you however I can."

"I need a friend."

"You got one."

Castle walked west on Terminal Avenue, head bent, shoulders tensed against the chill and the drizzle. There was the Canada Packers plant, its modern brick building. You could tell it was modern architecture because instead of being one big, solid brick block, it was a collection of smaller brick blocks that couldn't but make Castle think of them as afterthoughts; as if they'd just about finished the plant and some bright bulb remembered there were supposed to be employees' washrooms, and space for the typing pool, and so they added on more components. Some of these components were rounded on the ends that protruded from the main structure.

But whatever they did at Canada Packers in the interests of bright modernity was defeated by the piles of scrap wood and the heaps of iron pipe that were lying around in the mud. It was therefore somehow worse than the old forbidding nineteenth century buildings because those didn't make any false promises. And the old ones were just high enough to hide the chimney in the back lot. Castle thought of other chimneys, ones in Europe that many people preferred to pretend they didn't know about. And then there was the smell that the chimney belched forth to hang over Terminal Avenue. That too was like Europe.

CHAPTER EIGHT

Nine forty-five that night, Castle was standing at the intersection of Burrard and Davie Streets. The rain had stopped and he was looking in the plate glass windows of the auto dealership on the southeast corner, dreaming he had enough money to trade in his old Nash for one of these big, gleaming Laughlin Buicks. Hell, he wouldn't have the nerve to bring in the Nash. They'd just look at him like he was having his little joke: See what I brought back from the Demolition Derby. Want to trade? Hah, hah.

A taxi pulled to the curb and Little Joe Frontenac got out of the backseat. His black fedora, press pass in the band, was pushed back on his tousled head of thick black hair, knot in his knit tie pulled down and shirt unbuttoned at the collar.

"I don't know why this couldn't keep until morning," he said.

"And good evening to you too, Joe."

"So what's so important it can't wait?"

"You got ants in your pants, Joe?"

"Kind of. Listen, I found me a dame."

"You did?"

Castle was genuinely surprised.

"Anyway, Kilkenny told me some great stories but he's shy about letting me write about him. Says he has to think it over. I'm desperate, see."

"Yeah, you told me. So what does that have to do with…"

"Listen, so I go out to the strong women thing at the Kitsilano Pavillion."

"That's where you met your dame?"

"No, I met her a couple of days ago but I'm there watching all these muscle bound dames, a lot of them big deal diesel dykes, and when I get back, I knew I was hooked on my girl. She's such a tiny little doll. Only four foot eleven," the reporter said. "And she's Bulgarian."

"Is there a connection?"

"Funny guy."

"That's where you must have been last night when I called you after the cops nabbed me."

"Well to tell the truth…"

"You wouldn't want to do that."

"We went out to Maple Ridge."

"Why the hell would you do that?"

"We went to a Motor Court."

"Okay, if you insist on telling all about it, do so as we walk up the stairs to the studio."

"Where we going?"

"I just told you. Up the stairs to the studio."

"Don't be such a smartypants."

"That's it."

"What's it?"

"Mister Smartypants. We're going up to see Mister Smartypants. He's becoming part of the language. Louise is on the show tonight. She'll be done in a few minutes. As you were saying."

"We spent three days in the Motor Court last night."

"That's an old gag, Joe. You trying to tell me, she's a hot

number? This little miss, what's her name?"

"Ludmilla."

"And she's only four-foot eleven? With a name like that sounds like she should have been out there in Kits."

"She's very sophisticated. Speaks six languages. And can talk dirty in all of them. The things I could tell you."

"Well don't. My advice to you is save your strength. You're going to need it on account of I got an assignment for you."

"Oh, an assignment for me. Thanks a lot. I should remind you, I have a regular job with lots of pressure."

"Yeah, I know all about the pressure you're under. Turning out two columns a week. There's fellows pulling rickshaws in Shanghai would envy that kind of drudgery. Luftwaffe pilots have to bomb entire cities and be back in the barracks before curfew. Guys in hobo camps with kidnapped daughters."

"What's that?"

"Listen, this assignment offers some award-winning material for you."

"So give with it."

"After we meet Louise."

They went through the CACE door and into the radio station's reception area. A woman was sitting on a leather chair near the desk with her legs crossed, skirt half way up her thighs. The woman looked up in time to see Frontenac nudge Castle. She smirked, asked if she could be of any assistance.

"You sure can," said Frontenac, giving her the once over, from tip of the red-painted nails that poked from her open-toed sling-back sandals to the top of her bottle-blond head. "Miss, Miss…?"

She stood up and looked down on Joe Frontenac.

"Miss Szirtes."

Frontenac blushed.

"Are you the receptionist?"

"No, I read the news. Are you the messenger boy?"

"No, I'm Frontenac of the *Times*. I write the 'I Was There' column."

"Oh, I read that," Miss Szirtes said, and when she said it, Frontenac recovered, asked her if she liked the column.

"Oh, I do. You sure get up to some adventures, don't you?"

"'Deed I do. I bet we could get up to some adventures of our own."

"I bet we could too," said Miss Szirtes. "Why don't you call me when you reach your full height?"

She turned to Castle.

"I like a man who's big enough to fight back. Know what I mean?"

"Yeah, doll. I do." She was a doll too. He wondered where she would have gotten that brassiere under her sweater. Some place where they made them out of metal, it must be. She had a fetching beauty mark on the bridge of her nose.

"My girl friend feels the same way," Castle added. "That's her in there with Mister Smartypants."

"Oh, Louise Jones, the actress. I'd figure a girl like that would have a guy like you. You may wait for her in the control room if you wish. They're almost done. Take junior with you."

Frontenac, his attention on the floor, followed Castle out of the reception area.

"Thinks she's hot stuff, that broad," Frontenac said. Castle opened the door to the control room. "Just because she's got that great body. Did you get a load of her legs?"

"Shhh!" The engineer looked at them, pointed to a couple of chairs.

The guy leaned over his board of levers and knobs and toggle switches, staring through the glass and into the studio. Castle put on a pair of headphones. Louise was seated next to a fat man with round glasses; another woman sat off to the side of Louise at a telephone, receiver to her ear. The man saying, "Louise Jones will be off to the Esquimalt base on Vancouver Island tomorrow. And won't our troops be glad to see her. Louise?"

"Yes, Mister Smartypants?"

"I have a question for you."

"Fire away, Mister Smartypants."

"If I did, Louise. Would it be called a broadside?"

"Only if you hit what you were aiming for."

The engineer flicked a switch and the room filled with laughter. Held the switch down for two seconds, let go and there was no more laughter to be heard.

"No, seriously, Louise. Here's my question. Ah…"

"The answer is no."

More laughter.

"Now Mister Smartypants," Louise taking a piece of paper from the woman on the telephone. "From now on, I ask the questions. This one's from Missus Wanda Griffiths of West Sixth Avenue in our town."

"Okay, Louise," Mister Smartypants looking up at the clock. "Our last question of the evening."

Miss Szirtes entered the studio and sat at another desk with a microphone, lined up three sheets of paper in front of her.

"Mrs. Griffiths asks if you know the meaning of the word Triskaidekaphobia. That's spelled…"

"Fear of the number thirteen," said the fat man and looked toward the control room. The producer held up ten fingers and flashed them three times.

"I see we have time for one more quick question, Louise. Stump Mister Smartypants and you win twenty-five dollars."

"Here's one from Gene Castle of Cordova Street, our city."

"Gene Castle?" said Mister Smartypants.

"Yes. Mister Castle wants to know if you know the name of the Vancouver man who was the hero of the valiant Sandinista battle against the American troops who invaded Nicaragua in 1926."

Louise got up from the table and moved to a microphone stand at the centre of the room.

"That's an easy one Louise. Sorry, Gene Castle of Cordova

Street. You don't get your twenty-five dollars tonight. The answer is Alfred 'Red' Batson who, by the way, wrote a very good book about his adventures called *Vagabond's Paradise*. That's all the time we have for questions tonight, folks. This is CACE, Your Ace of Stations, and I'm Mister Smartypants. It's a big world out there and I hope you'll take the time to learn some more about it. Now, here's Louise Jones to sing us out of here with 'I'll Be Seeing You,' followed by the lovely Robyn Szirtes reading the ten o'clock news."

Castle listened while Louise did her song, and then he removed the earphones. She looked up at the window and pointed with her finger which he took to mean she'd meet him in the reception area. He nodded and as he stood up, he noticed Miss Szirtes leaning forward on the edge of her chair, so far forward that she appeared to have a sway back. That posture served to show her posterior rounded in a most delightful manner. He saw her lips moving silently over the microphone. When he turned away, he noticed Joe Frontenac was also noticing.

Louise came into the reception area as self-contained as ever. No physical indication that she had just sung on a live radio broadcast. "Mister S-P'll be out in a moment. He claims he knows you and you're going to be surprised. You threw him for a loop with that last question."

"What's his real name?"

"Let him tell you."

"What's the dish on the blonde dame?" Frontenac asked Louise.

"Forget it, Joe. She'd eat you up and spit you out."

"She already did," Castle said.

"I wouldn't mind," Frontenac said. "They get to know me, they get to overlook my, well, you know."

"Overlook is the word," muttered Louise.

"My God, though. She's the most fantastic dame I've seen since—. Ah, no offense, Louise, but I don't know since when. Maybe since forever. I…"

"Not this again, Joe," Castle said. "Early this year it was the singer from the Porters' Retreat. Back in '37 there was the girl in Spain, combing her hair at the mirror hung on the olive tree in that little town. I remember there was the girl worked at Garmano's and, before that, well, I didn't know you before that. But it must have gone on before that."

The door opened and Mister Smartypants appeared, forehead shiny with sweat, black-rimmed glasses all misty. He smiled at Castle and extended a short-fingered pudgy hand. "Yeah, yeah. You don't recognize me. I'm not offended."

"I'm sorry, Mister Smartypants. I don't. You look familiar though."

The man shook his big head. His hair was curly and oily. He took off his glasses and began cleaning them with his handkerchief. "You share a chicken coop for three days with another guy and you think he'd remember. We smelled so bad the chickens wouldn't come home to roost."

"It can't be."

"Yeah, it is. Three guys pinned down in a goddamned Nicaraguan swamp with bullets flying overhead, you'd think everybody would remember each other for the rest of their lives. I bet the other guy, Alfred 'Red' Batson would remember. I thought that was why you asked Mister Smartypants that question."

"Arnold Hanratty the Third."

"Why, no, Gene," Louise interjected. "That's not his name."

The fat man nodded his head vigorously, his chin doubling itself on the downward motion.

"It used to be, Louise. But we shan't refer to it again. I'm Cecil Krebs now."

Krebs sniffed and blinked, and Castle saw his eyes get misty. He looked at the fat man and wondered how it could be. His mind went into high gear searching for a resemblance to the man he had lived alongside for practically a year in those wild days in that beautiful country.

"It must have been what?" Castle asked. "Fourteen, fifteen

years?"

"I tell you exactly how long it was," Krebs said. "It was exactly one hundred and thirty-five pounds ago."

"You were always reading."

"Still am always reading."

"You had a tattoo," Castle said.

"And you were there when I got it. You and Red."

He saw Joe Frontenac bring his spiral notebook from the inside jacket of his pocket, and added. "Look, my friend here's a reporter."

Krebs eyes darted to Frontenac and the look in the guy's eyes was somehow familiar. His expression changed, features going blank. It was the fighter's look.

"I'm Frontenac of the *Times*."

Frontenac held out his hands. Krebs didn't take it.

"He's a reporter but he won't write anything you don't want him to write. He's good people. We've been through a spot or two of trouble together ourselves."

Krebs nodded and shook Frontenac's hand.

"Glad to meet you. One story you won't be writing is the shady past of Mister Smartypants."

"I gotcha."

The fat man turned back to Castle.

"I still have it. The tattoo."

"I beg your pardon, Louise," Mister Smartypants said, and unbuttoned his shirt. There on his wide smooth chest was a long-haired Latin American beauty in a ripped blouse, a bandielero slung over her shoulder and separating her breasts, in a long skirt slit all the way up to her thighs; she was gripping the pole of a flag with one hand while the other clasped the stock of a rifle. The flag was red and black, the anarchist colours.

"It is a thing of beauty," Louise said.

Mister Smartypants smiled. "Now, let's us all go get something to eat. If, after seeing that, you have any appetite. We'll grab a cab and head down to the Eden Café on Granville. I'm on the arm there and no one bothers me. The big problem with this job is I can't go anywhere without someone trying to stump me. Also at the Eden, we can get coffee with legs."

After the meal, they sat around drinking rum and coffee, catching up and swapping lies. Louise entertained them with anecdotes about her experiences at troop shows. Frontenac recounted highlights of some recent columns and Krebs told how he'd gotten from soldier of fortune to radio personality. He had done a three-year jolt back in Ontario and spent the time getting fat, reading encyclopedias and working on the prison radio station. After his release, he headed west, getting his training on stations in Port Arthur, Winnipeg and Saskatoon.

"Guy in Saskatoon wanted to know what was the use of knowing all that stuff. He meant like Tris Speaker's lifetime batting average, the etymology of the word 'terradiddle,' the name of Jakob Boheme's wife and the practice of infibulation throughout the world. He called it 'useless' information. So I decided to make it useful. To me anyway. I came up with the idea for the show, moved to Vancouver and sold it to CACE, your ace of stations. Too bad I can't talk about stuff like infibulation on the air."

"That reminds me," Castle said. "There's supposed to be some place in town that caters to the kind of people who might find those sorts of thing of interest."

Krebs nodded his head.

"You've heard about it?"

"Christ, Gene," Louise said. "You'd think you could wait until I left town."

"Smile when you say that, Louise."

He told them about Skinny O'Day's missing girl.

"Who'd steal a high class hooker unless it was somebody connected with a another brothel?"

"A jealous lover?" Louise said.

"Or both," Frontenac added.

"What I heard," Krebs said, "the place is in a factory or warehouse somewhere and it supplies what you want but can't get at a regular place, let alone at home unless coercion is employed."

"You mean," Frontenac asked, "like legless women, eunuchs, little girls?"

"Some people," Krebs said, "have little girls at home. Little boys too. Maybe some have eunuchs. But I also mean, this is just what I hear, corprophilia, even necrophilia."

Castle stopped listening. He heard them talk but he didn't listen. It didn't sound like the place for a beautiful young women from a Rossetti painting, even if she was a fallen angel. No, what got him was the part about the little girls.

Then he didn't want to think about that anymore so he turned his attention back to Krebs who was saying the place was, evidently, run by a woman.

"You know anything about this woman?"

"No."

"Is it her place or she is the front man, front woman?"

"Well, congratulations Gene Castle, of Cordova Street. You've just won twenty-five dollars because you stumped Mister Smartypants."

Out on the sidewalk, Mister Smartypants hailed a cab and asked if he could give anyone a lift. Joe Frontenac wanted to take him up on the offer but Castle grabbed his arm. The fat man shrugged and the cab took off.

"Hell'd you do that for? Can't bear to part from me?"

"That's it, Joe. Also, I haven't had the time to tell you your assignment. The one that is to provide you with several columns."

Frontenac pulled back the cuff of his jacket, checked his watch. "It better be good, Gene. Ludmilla's waiting up for me."

"You were nicer when you were celibate, Joe. But here's the deal."

Castle told him about the hobo camp, and how he wanted Frontenac to go and hang around for a few days.

"Dress like a 'bo. You don't want to look like a newspaper

reporter. Why, Joe I'll never forget the first time I paid attention to your column. This was before I met you, of course. You did that series of stories about what it was like to be on skidrow, sleeping on the street or in the missions, panhandling at back doors."

"Yes, I did capture the way it was. And you know why Gene?"

"Because you are the best hardnosed reporter of your era?"

"Well, there's that. But because I became one of them."

"Them?"

"Yes, a real down-and-out victim of the Depression."

"With a cozy apartment to come home to after the story was over, but never mind. This is a different kind of caper. They don't call them Knights of the Road for nothing. Why each of the men in this particular jungle is a story himself. Especially High-Line and Laramie Stribling. And there're others coming in and going out all the time. Trouble is somebody's a bad guy. And I think I know which one it is. Anyway, another one of them is a guy you met once and it was only the other day you told me you wished you could meet again."

"The other day?"

"In Ramona's."

"Hmm, the only person I mentioned was that fellow Leandro Martine, but you can't mean him, so you must be mistaken. Hey, wait…It can't be."

"Yeah, it is. But don't blow his gaff, Joe. Be cool."

"Oh, I will. I will! Man, this is great. Thanks, Gene."

"See you, Joe."

He took Louise's arm and they walked off.

"You really trust the little guy. Don't you, Gene?"

"He's proven himself, over and over again."

"Yeah, but he gets carried away sometimes and I got a feeling this Martine fellow's not to be messed with. What happens if Joe blows his cover?"

"Well, at least, in his last few days, he'll have had Ludmilla."

CHAPTER NINE

When the goddamned Russian alarm clock went off in the morning, sounding like a cross between the Kronstadt Mutiny and the Spike Jones Orchestra, Castle was curled into Louise's back. He had been dreaming of Seville, the narrow little streets, a weekend there stolen from the war. Louise moaned and Castle turned over, reached out blindly to hammer the clock with the heel of his hand. "Seven-thirty already," Louise groaned.

Only then did Castle open his eyes. It was dark, as dark as when they'd gone to sleep. "What?" he caught himself muttering it, all confused, his mind stumbling around in the dark.

Louise gave him a "What?" back and when she opened her eyes, declared the goddamned alarm clock must have betrayed them, it couldn't be more than two in the morning. But Castle lit a match and read the clock face. Seven-thirty two. He got out of bed and went over to the window, rolled up the shade. There were cars and trucks creeping along Cordova Street, their headlights on.

"What's going on?" Louise called.

"There's a pea souper out there and if a fellow didn't know

119

about the peat fires on Lulu Island and the beehive burners along False Creek, a fellow would think the whole west end had gone up in flames and the smoke had blown over here to strangle us."

Louise got out of bed and came over to the window for a look.

"It is the kind of day where people get up to all sorts of things."

"I feel like getting up to one sort of thing."

"Me, too, baby. I'd like to try on the WREN outfit again and this time you wouldn't have to take it off me. But, alas, I have a bus to catch."

"You didn't have to remind me. Of either."

They stepped out onto the pavement half an hour later. Deep South Durkins was in his usual spot, just beginning his first number. At least, the sound was coming from the same spot. They couldn't see him, just hear about the little girl lost somewhere in the fogs of memory.

"We need a couple of kerosene lamps," Louise said.

"I haven't seen one this bad since I was a kid. Went somewhere with my dad once. I remember him feeling in the dark for the numbers, for the address of a house."

"All the lights are on in all the stores that are open," Louise said. "It is kind of romantic, in an eerie way."

"Yeah, it's romantic as hell."

They walked through the dark to Ramona's. Guy and Raymond were at the counter; Matty Muldoon, the young sad-eyed hooker who'd been looking at Castle a few days ago was at a booth in the back. Maybe she was just getting off work.

Louise barely had time for a coffee. They said goodbye with a quick kiss and she was gone. Into a cab and to the Pacific Coach Lines bus station. She'd be away two nights and three days, the troupe breaking in their show at the base in Abbotsford in the Fraser Valley before heading to Esquimalt on the Island.

Maude came around to fill up his cup and complain about

the fog and the smoke, and Castle thought about going out into it, looking for a missing hooker and a missing twelve-year-old girl, and didn't like the prospect so he ordered breakfast.

"Stack of two with a blinded pair!" Maude hollered in the direction of the unseen Tommy Chew. She moved away and the space where she'd been was filled or partly filled by the young hooker with the sad-eyes.

"May I sit? My name is Edith."

"Well since it's Edith, you may sit. But if it were something else, like Gloria or Hortense, there's no way I could let you occupy that bench seat."

"I was told you had a funny way of talking."

"Who told you that?"

"A couple of people. Most recent one told me just last night."

"Oh, yeah? And who might that be?"

"Mister Smartypants."

"We're old friends."

"So I have heard."

The girl, she couldn't have been more than twenty-two, looked like the street but she didn't talk street.

"Where were you educated, if I might ask?"

"You just did." She smiled. He could tell because of the way she curled the left corner of her mouth. "I was educated at a convent. We studied theology and the classics."

"What's your last name?"

"Wilton. Edith Wilton. At least, that's the name I took when I left."

"Were you taken there as a baby like your namesake was?"

She looked at him with astonishment. "You got the reference."

"'Knowing not the world,'" Castle said, "'rather than forsaking it.'"

For a moment her eyes lost their cynicism as she stared at him. Then she pursed her lips in a grimace.

"When I was eighteen I forsook the convent for the world. And I got more than I reckoned on. Of course, one of the reasons I left the convent in the first place was to get away from one nun in particular who had an intense curiosity about what I had under my skirts."

"You know," Castle said. "I just remembered you."

"What? You sneaked into the convent to get a look yourself?"

"I'm not that daring."

"If you wanted a look now, I'm afraid you would have to pay."

"I don't think so. I mean, I don't think I'd do that."

"I didn't think so either but I had to ask. It is kind of like a habit. Pardon the pun."

"I got that, too. You used to dye your hair black, meet your *maquereu* at the Anchor Tavern."

"Thanks right. But I don't meet him anymore."

"Why? Somebody send him to his reward?"

"Yes, and I was the one. And I only did eighteen months for it. In New Westminster."

"I heard the woman's wing is worse than the men's."

"You heard right."

"So how do you know Mister Smartypants?"

"I was hooking independent or trying too. But I was always getting recruited, you know, by pimps. I had a few regulars and the main one was Mister Smartypants. He advanced me some money and I got off the stroll. The other girls made fun of him, Mister Smartypants, because he's so fat. They used to say, he looks like a guy who's just come back from the beach, stole all the little kids beachballs and is trying to hide them under his clothes."

"That's not nice."

"No, but he is. He pays the rent and I never charge him. I cook him meals sometimes."

"You are, indeed, a saint."

"I make it up with my others. I got this one guy, he makes

122

me dress up like Ronnie Foster. You know who she is?"

"Yeah, I saw her picture in the paper. The Bren Gun Girl of the Year."

"He saw her picture too, the guy I told you about, and fell for her cute button nose, cute tongue poking out as she bends to her work riffling barrels to smooth the bullets on their way."

"Into the bodies of some German mothers' sons."

"Why, Mister Castle. You can get in trouble talking like that."

"Not in here, sweetheart."

"Anyway, my client wore out her picture, if you get my meaning so he came and found me. He calls when he's ready and I get into my dungarees and plaid shirt, turn the collar up, wrap my hair in a scarf like Ronnie Foster, or Aunt Jemima, and I'm there waiting for him. Have to stick my tongue out just so. Man, when the gentleman sees me like that he attacks me like Alicibiades did Syracuse."

"That's quite a picture Edith but what, if anything, does it have to do with the price of bananas?"

"The gentleman, when he first came to call, related his troubles trying to get someone to satisfy his desires. They either wouldn't go along with him or were never the right types. Then he heard about a place where they cater to a person's particular twist. He contacted them but was turned down. What he wants, they tell him, is too tame."

"I've been hearing rumours about that place."

"Yes, well, this same gentleman used to go to Skinny O'Day's establishment and he knows the girl with the red hair who is missing, but she's only missing if you're Skinny O'Day. She now works at the place where they cater to dastardly perversions and she's the owner's pet. And the owner is big and mean."

"Who is he?"

"It, and I use the word purposely, is not a he."

"Well where is this house of wonders?"

"I don't know."

"So when's the next time you do your Ronnie Foster imitation?"

"Next time he needs his barrel riffled. Should be any day now. I'll let you know."

It was still dark outside although getting on to ten o'clock in the morning. The smoke from the peat fires mingled with the fog and wrapped everybody and everything in its damp brown scarf. Well, one good thing about this brown world, Castle told himself, is that it is a relief from gray. When you live in this usually sodden town you get to know plenty about Gray. Must be, he told himself, sort of like eskimos and snow. Up there north of Frobisher Bay, fellow probably comes out of his igloo, his house of skins of a morning, says, "Oh, it is not the big flat snowflakes like stars today but the little mean-looking ones." Whereas, a fellow like me would only see Snow.

But I got that eskimo fellow beat when it comes to gray. Usually, by which I mean eight straight months of the year and parts of the others, the sky is generally a Dishwater Gray. Though, often, when it is real nasty or getting there, it looks to be a sort of Pewter Gray. Every once in awhile, thank heavens, the gray heavens for that, it is a sort of galvanized Washtub Gray that makes you think, or hope, that there is a sun somewhere behind, waiting to spill out over the sides. Then there is the worst of all, what'd you'd call or I'd call a Phlegm Gray.

Yes, Castle continued, so Brown is a relief and I say that only because, as all my friends would agree, I am an optimist, a positive kind of fellow, always trying to look at the sunny side of things, as it were or isn't.

One can't make out very much of anything today. Though in the tunnels made by automobile headlights and in the halo of streetlamps, you can see the weave of the scarf, spooky brown tangled threads of peat and fog. Also, concentrating, one becomes aware of the vague shapes of things, humps of automobile hoods and fenders, the vertical shafts of buildings. Anyway this was his beat so Castle knew the vertical shaft up ahead and to the left was the building that housed the daily newspaper in Mandarin and that the voice he heard belonged to Woody his humpbacked pal, an Indian hawking newspapers in English on a Chinese corner. He knew further that the corner directly over the way, the Shanghai Alley corner, was also Chinese despite the Orange Crush sign in the grocery store window that he couldn't see but imagined in his mind. He also imagined that he could make out, in the glow of a streetlamp, at least one Chinese character on a rooming house sign, imagined some old man with a long beard drawing the character with his brush, a respectful student looking over his shoulder, amazed by his deft stroke, learned over decades in the old country.

"Nazi Peace Terms Handed to France!"

"Hey there, Woody."

"Whosit? Gene? Is that you?"

"Yeah."

"Where are you? I can't see a damn thing."

Castle reached out and touched the man.

"Touch my hump for luck, Gene; then maybe this stuff will blow away."

"I like it, it's kind of romantic. Makes me feel like Sherlock Holmes."

"Makes me feel like shit; yeah, Sherlock Shit, if you'll pardon the expression. Say, you know about this outfielder down in Spokane, this Smead Jolley?"

"Guy hits all the homeruns?"

"Yeah. Well, he hit three yesterday against Tacoma. Only thing is, he can't catch a cold, not even in this weather. He got beaned. In the outfield. Settled under a pop fly that my aunt Annie Joseph could catch. Fifty games into the season he has thirty homeruns and about the same number of errors."

"Maybe you should call it out, Woody. Keep the world in

perspective."

"Good idea. Here's your paper."

Castle ran his hand from the tough cartilage of Woody's hump down his arm to the paper, and told him he'd see him later.

Castle turned to his left because he knew in that direction lay his office, and Woody cried, "Nazi Peace Terms Handed to France! ... Smead Jolley hits three, drops three! ... Read all about it!"

He looked up and looked all around and found no relief from the brown but then he looked down and he could see the ground. Stepping off the curb, he saw asphalt that was, alas, gray, but a dark sort of charcoal gray. And, lo and behold, there were patches where the asphalt had worn away revealing old cobblestones. No sense looking up, Castle told himself, so he continued looking down as he crossed the street, searching for more reminders of days long gone when his old man would have strolled along cobblestone streets and horse and buggies come rattling along, passengers and drivers jiggling up and down.

He was thus engaged, about to break into a few verses of "A Surrey with the Fringe on Top," when he heard a pop like a champagne cork and looked up into the brown thinking there was a party going on, and what in the world could they be celebrating. There was another pop and it was as if this second cork hit him in the arm. They must be standing real close, Castle thought. Don't they have any manners, never point the bottle at a fellow. Then a patch of cobblestone was rushing up at him, and there was another pop.

"Hello, Sister."

"Hello, my son. Welcome back."

"Where've I been?"

"In the land of dreams."

"Where am I?"

"In the hospital."

"What's the matter with my arm?"

"You were shot. Don't you remember?"

"No, I thought I heard champagne corks."

"Those were just in your dreams. You were shot through the left arm but you are very fortunate."

"Thank you. I always feel fortunate when I'm shot."

"Oh, you're such a wise guy, it must be the drugs."

"No, Sister. I'm always like this. How long have I been here?"

"Since yesterday morning. Twenty-six hours."

"Jesus! —You're supposed to tell me not to say that."

"Don't take the Lord's name in vain, my son."

"I won't if you promise not to call me your son. Especially since I'm older than you."

"Deal."

"I've seen you before."

"Yes, you have. About a year ago. Then it was a knife wound. According to the records you've been here quite a few times but that was the first time I saw you. I'm Sister Marie Gorelli."

"Sister."

"I was telling some of the girls that things sure would be slow around here if it wasn't for you."

"Well, keep it in mind. Treat me nice or I'm liable to take my trade over to the competition."

She was a nice looking woman, wearing the surplice but nothing on her head. She had short black hair. Kind of reminded him of Louise Brooks.

"Where's my pal, Saint Camillus?"

"He's in the hallway where he's been these many decades. Our patron."

"I need that drink. Remember you said if I ever needed a drink, I should come see you?"

Sister Marie leaned over the bed to speak, "We'll have to

wait for that. There're some people here to see you."

"Hey! We'll have none of that whispering."

"With a growl like that I knew it had to be you, Horace."

The Chief of Detectives was there on the sister's left.

"It's Chief Koronicki to you."

"Well if it's Chief Koronicki, this must be business."

"You're goddamned right it is. Two dead bodies and you're the link between them. Now somebody takes a shot at you. Three shots according to the redskin."

"You got peculiar friends, Castle."

Now Detective Bartoli was in his view, edging Sister Marie out of the picture. Castle moved his head to the left but there was a stab of pain that spread over his skull like ripples in water. He moved his eyes to the left, caught a peripheral glimpse of her but that hurt too. It was only then that he became aware that his head was bandaged.

"I asked you a question, Castle."

"No, you didn't, Danny. You made a comment about my friends."

"Don't call me by my first name. Only my friends call me by my first name."

"I kind of thought, once upon a time, that you and I could be friends."

"That's before I knew much about you. Didn't know about your friends. Reds and redskins."

"Don't forget hobos, tramps, rounders, some double amputees, a Sikh or two, a one-armed wrestler, couple or three dwarfs, and I used to know a midget Rumanian juggler, nice guy name of Tiny Tedescu. Guess you wouldn't approve of them either."

"Don't get smart with me, Castle!"

"Or, what?"

"Or, I'll take a piece out of your hide. Cut your reputation down to size."

"What the hell has gotten into you, Danny? I mean,

Bartoli?"

"It is not so much what's gotten into him," said a female voice, "as what he hasn't gotten into. And ain't ever going to get into."

There was Laura Easely walking past Bartoli and around the foot of the bed to the other side. She sat down on a white chair, placed a hand on Castle's right one and glared at the detective who glared right back.

"Is that your mean, scary look, Danny?" Laura asked him.

Danny glowered at her.

"No, Laura," Castle said. "That's the cop academy look."

Bartoli made a move toward Castle, but his boss blocked him with a hip.

"What's the matter with you, Danny? You going to take a poke at him? Let him sue you? You're in court his lawyer says, 'Is it true that when you hit Mister Castle, he was in bed in the hospital with a concussion and a gunshot wound, getting plasma or whatever the fuck it is, put in his arm?' And then they call the other witnesses. One of them a goddamned nun."

"Maybe," said Laura, "he'll give me and the Sister that fierce look, try and scare us off."

"It won't work, Laura," Castle said. "You're too tough. Might work on the schoolyard though, whenever the detective's short of lunch money."

"You're going to get up out of that bed one of these days," Bartoli said. "And I'll be waiting."

"Thanks. You just threatened me in front of the same two witnesses."

Bartoli turned around and stalked out of the room.

"That's desertion of duty, Koronicki."

The Chief shook his head.

"You might have pushed it too far, Gene. He's a tough kid. And he's your size. And he's a lot younger."

"I got enough to worry about. Somebody shot me."

"You got any ideas who it might have been?"

"No, I was walking along minding my own business."

"What are you working on now?"

"A missing person's case."

"Who's the person?"

"Can't tell you."

"Why doesn't the client come to us?"

Castle managed something between a laugh and a grunt. It hurt his head.

"All right. Forget I asked."

"I think he needs to rest now," said Marie Gorelli.

"All right, Sister, I'm going."

All three watched him leave.

"I could use that drink now, Sister."

Marie Gorelli nodded, "I'll go see to that."

Castle looked at Laura's hand that was on top of his hand, then he looked questioningly at her.

"So what happened between you and Bartoli?"

Laura moved her hand. "Well, you know, I fell for him. Or for his looks, anyway. My crush lasted until he started talking. He calls me, asked to come over. I said, all right. He was in a foul mood, said he'd been to the trainyards and found a dead body and seen you there, and had some words with you. He started bad mouthing you and I told him to get out. He said, What's the matter? The guy putting it to you on the side? I told him to do something that would be difficult if not impossible to accomplish, then he laughed and grabbed me, started massaging my breasts like he was polishing a squad car. I told him to stop, he didn't so I stomped on the top of his foot with my shoe. The four inch heel of the shoe that I'd put on just for him. Only for a different reason. He cursed me something fierce, called me a dyke and got out of there."

"Charming first date, that."

"First and last."

"Whatever happened with you and Art Sprague?"

Laura shook her head.

"I see Bartoli, he talks about you. I go out with Art, he talks about Louise. Only he likes Louise a hell of a lot more than Bartoli likes you. I got sick of Louise-this, Louise-that. I don't know, Gene. Art has a habit of getting what he wants. Maybe he doesn't go after it directly, he lays back and waits but he gets it. And Louise. Maybe she's getting to where she wants something a little more, I don't know, settled or something."

"Louise? You kidding? We're almost a, well, a tradition."

"Yeah, and sometimes what a tradition is, is just something from the past, a habit that has a way of turning into a memory."

Before Castle could respond, Sister Marie came in the room, plates, utensils and glasses rattling around on the tray she carried in front of her.

"I see an invalid's lunch on there, Marie. Tea, toast, bowl of soup. What's under that other lid, some nice oatmeal?"

"You're close. It is also made from grain."

She took out the bottle of rye, poured some in a glass for Castle, pointed a glass at Laura.

"No, thanks Sister. I have to go to work."

Laura stood up, said, "See you, Gene," and started to go. Then she stopped, took a deep breath, exhaled, bent over the bed and kissed him on the lips.

Sister Marie looked at her with surprise but not as much surprise as Castle.

"I've been wanting to do that for ten years," Laura said, as she went out the door.

"What did she mean by that? Ten years she hasn't kissed you? Isn't she your girl?"

"No, she's not."

"Well she kissed you like she is."

"Yes, she did."

They touched glasses and drank. Sister Marie seemed to get another one poured and driank before she could possibly have swallowed the first.

"Damn, sister. You had those two so quickly they probably hit together on the way down."

She smiled, bit her lower lip.

"Ten years."

"Ten years, what?"

"That girl. Wanting to kiss someone for ten years and finally doing it. I've wanted to kiss someone for about twenty years now."

"You've been carrying a torch all that long, sister? Who's the fellow?"

"Any fellow. I've been wanting to kiss a man all these years. To see what it's like."

"You mean, you've never kissed a guy?"

"Oh, when I was a kid. I was fifteen the last time. But that was a boy. I've never kissed a man."

She finished the drink. Bit her lip as she looked at him. Castle knew what was coming even though he didn't believe it. But when Sister Marie poured herself another one, he thought he was mistaken. She knocked it back, banged the glass down on the bedside table, placed her warm hands very gently on either side of his head, very gently, and kissed him on the lips, the way she'd seen Laura do it.

It only lasted a couple of seconds. Castle didn't move, couldn't move. He watched her draw back and look toward the door, then she licked her lips and kissed him again. Longer this time, and Castle thought, it must be instinct. Some of them have it and some of them don't. You can't learn it, really, and you don't lose it once you have it. Sister Marie ran her tongue over his lips and pulled away.

She stood straight. Smoothed her habit with her hands. She was trembling.

"There are two pills on the tray. Take them and they'll help you sleep."

"If I'm going to sleep, I'll need the help. I'm certainly wide awake now."

"I think I better leave. Or I'm liable to do something else I've always wanted to do and have never done. Even when I was fifteen. God help me."

She crossed herself and got out of there.

Castle took his two pills. He wanted to shake his head at the wonder of it all but his head hurt too much. Curious, it hadn't hurt when Sister Marie Gorelli kissed him or when Laura kissed him. Castle thought about Louise over on the Island, entertaining the troops. Honestly, Louise I did nothing to encourage them. In fact, seeing how I couldn't even move, let alone fight them off, the hussies took advantage of me.

He settled back against the pillows. Ah, it was all right being in the hospital. A relief from the streets. The pillows were oh, so soft. He would just close his eyes for a moment.

Castle and Louise were walking across the back lot. She had a satin robe thrown over her skimpy sequined and spangled outfit and he was vined down, done up in his gaudiest jacket, cream-coloured, pleated pants and brown and white kicks with spats. For some reason, he had a derby on his head. It was Tiny Nichol's Wonder Shows, encamped in a muddy lot at the edge of town. The town was either Peterborough, Ontario or Perpignon, France. Castle was pointing out to Louise how the mud covered his brown-and-whites and then just rolled off them. "See they're as shiny as new. It's my latest invention, the new miracle coating I was telling you about. I'll sell it to every carnie spieler and circus barker in the world. All I need's a moneybags."

Just then they heard laughter and saw, between the tents, a townie perched atop a pile of white granules, salt or sugar or cocaine. He was holding out handfuls of bills. "I'll invest!" said the man, and Castle knew he should recognize him. "I'll just take Louise as collateral."

"Don't be ridiculous. Louise and me are in this together."

The man gave a knowing look and disappeared.

"Anyway, Louise. What with my reversible private eye raincoats and my fedoras with the bullet holes already in them, I'll make a fortune. We'll make a fortune together, Louise. 'Cause, yes, we're in this together."

"You're not kidding, Gene!"

And they began to sing. "We're in this together!"

They sang as they walked, mud sliding off Gene's shoes, spangles shimmying on Louise's brassiere, and other members of the show took up the song, "Together! Together! We're in this together!"—the roughies and the ride boys, the rag head and the rubber man, a chorus line of kooch girls, the fat lady and the pinhead, and even the geek were singing, or trying to—"Together! Together! We're in this together!"

The whole damn show or most of it had raised its voice in song by the time Gene and Louise reached the midway. Suddenly Leandro Martine, in a clown's suit fashioned from the blue mono of the Spanish anarchists, was there beside them, and just as they were about to turn the corner at the Ten-In-One they spotted three who weren't singing. There was a girl with kohl eyes and rubbery breasts, her skin covered in coconut oil. "Nymph," said Leandro Martine, "in thy orisons be all my sins remembered."—She laughed lasciviously and began to pull on her nipples. The other woman was taller than Castle, dressed in a loin cloth, her stomach seemed to be made of rolling pins, her arms of ropes, the left one extended over her head, and in her hand she supported Teddy Tedescu, the Rumanian midget, only he was dressed in a cowboy outfit and firing his cap pistol into the air above Peterborough or Perpignon. The Nymph began to make like Little Egypt, pressing her belly into Leandro, then rubbing a hip against his hip. The big woman scowled, set Teddy Tedescu down on the ground and grabbed the cap pistol out of his hand. It turned into a long Colt revolver and Castle recognized it as the one Annie Oakley had given to Laramie Stribling. Then the big woman with the muscles emptied all six bullets into Leandro Martine. As the smoke from the powder cleared, Castle noticed the little girl staring from a rent in the canvas of the Ten-In-One tent. Her eyes were made up to look like those of the Nymph covered in coconut oil. The big woman threw the gun down in the mud and started moving toward Castle.

"There, there! It's all right now. Everything is all right."

A large dark skinned man had his hands on Castle's shoulders and was pressing him firmly back against the pillows. Sister Marie Gorelli with her hands folded, saying, "You just had a bad dream is all."

The man wore a turban and for a moment Castle thought he was still dreaming and the Sikh was part of it. But then he understood, or thought he did, and uttered an intelligent, "Uh."

The sister gave Castle another pill and a glass of water and when he settled back, she saw to sticking the intravenous tube back into his arm. The orderly arranged Castle's bedclothes, folded the sheet back down over the blanket. Pretty decent of him, Castle thought. Marie pressed the flat of her hand against Castle's forehead and smiled at him. Castle saw the Sikh look at her curiously. Then they were gone and he retreated to the land of dreams, of sweet dreams this time.

CHAPTER TEN

The next morning Castle managed to dress himself with help from neither nun nor Sikh. The most difficult part was getting the trenchcoat to drape over his shoulders. Sister Marie came in the room as he was about to leave.

"Don't you ever have any time off, sister?"

"The Lord's work is never done, my son."

"Yeah, yeah."

"There's a handsome hobo fellow waiting for you at the reception area, and I wanted to see you on your way. Also, we may never meet again. Then, on the other hand, given your record, you'll probably be back before too long."

"Let's go by my old pal, Saint Camillus, on the way out."

Saint Camillus was in his familiar place in a frame at the end of the hall. Castle gave him a nod.

"He's a tough old son of a gun, eh Marie?"

Camillus had long white hair and beard, his face lined and seamed, his nose twisted. He looked Walt Whitman's twin brother who'd chosen pugilism over poetry.

"Yes, Gene. And the way you're going, a few more scars, you'll look just like him."

"Thanks sister."

When they reached the lobby, Castle recognized Frontenac with a three-day's growth of beard, chewing on an unlighted cigar, sprawled in a chair, legs stretched before him, the way he figured a genuine hobo might do it. He was dressed in old Army clothes, boots too; familiar fedora stuck on his head.

"If it isn't Deadline Joe, King of the Bos."

Frontenac sighed, "Should have known I couldn't fool you."

"Almost, Joe. It was the hat just-so on your head of tousled hair. The dirt smeared on your cheeks is a good touch too."

"Damn it, Gene. I didn't smear dirt... Oh, sorry, sister."

"You are forgiven my son. You are merely human. All too human."

Sister Marie assumed a look of piety, standing four-square against evil's relentless onslaught.

"Your disguise," Castle said to her, "is better than Joe's."

"What?" said Frontenac.

"Never mind."

"You've got me wrong, Gene," said Sister Marie. "I like a drink now and again, and my mind may be haunted by bad thoughts, but I do believe."

"Good for you sister. You're lucky."

"I'll see you, Gene. Maybe under other circumstances."

"I got stuff to tell you," Frontenac said when they were out under a pale blue sky.

"Let's walk."

Castle leaned his head back to absorb some of the sun, weak but sun nevertheless.

"You hurt your neck, too?"

"No, sir. What I'm doing here is paying attention to the gifts from heaven."

"That Sister in there is having her influence on you."

"You might say that."

"What're you going to do when we get down Burrard Street a ways, near the little park there? You going to smell the flowers?"

"Maybe."

"Yeah, you bend over the flower beds, that's the time the guys with the guns will come by again. It'll give me good material. Something about maybe you knew your time had come so you were picking your own flowers for around your final resting place."

"How about 'Impatiens to be Going?'"

"That's good."

"You can have it. Now what's the scoop?"

"Fry Pan. He's the rat."

"I figured either him or Weyburn Willie."

"Weyburn hit the road. Fry Pan leaves the jungle to meet with some Italian or Greek guy. The guy gives him money sometimes."

"How often do they meet?"

"Couple of times a day."

"Where?"

"Never more than a five minute walk from the camp. Sometimes along Terminal Avenue. Sometimes down at the bus station."

"Any other places?"

"No, either one or the other."

"Is there a pattern to the meets?"

"I never thought about it like that."

"That's because you don't think like a wily private eye."

"I guess not. But, come to think of it, I guess they alternate. Mornings at the bus station. Late afternoons along the street."

"Good work, Joe. What else you got for me?"

"Nothing except it sure is interesting around that jungle. All the stories those guys tell. Except Leandro. He doesn't say much. Pretends not to speak much English. Says he speaks French. None of the rest of them speak French. We, he and I, don't talk

French so's not to get Fry Pan suspicious."

"Leandro know about Fry Pan?"

"Yeah."

"You ask him why Mr. Fry Pan is still living?"

"Yeah, he said if he'd killed him then I wouldn't have discovered he meets some Italian or Greek guy. Or maybe he's Portuguese. Reminds me a little bit of that cop, Bartoli."

"That's because they all look alike those Italians. And Greeks. Portuguese, too."

"I know what you mean."

"What else you got for me?"

"Leandro told me about his work. Ever since the Nazis started their road trip through Europe, he's been sneaking into the countries that have been overrun, establishing connections with people interested in resistance, attempting to get things organized. Everybody trying to get out, he's trying to get in. Says it is better to link up all these groups in France, in Norway, in Belgium, in Poland so people don't think they're alone."

"He's a brave son-of-a-gun."

"And he sure respects you, Gene. Felt real bad you got gunned down and that it's probably to do with him."

"Yeah, so I suppose we ought to come up with a plan."

"We? You're the boss. While you're thinking of something ingenious, I'll tell you something I saw. One of these peripheral things incidental to the situation at hand but curious nevertheless. Being an ace reporter, I have an eye for these sorts of things, and…"

"So what is it, already?"

"I'm always working. Always on the lookout, eh?"

"Being an ace reporter."

"Yeah, yeah. Remember I told you about the lady weightlifters?"

"Uh huh."

"Well the day before yesterday, the weather had cleared when I woke at dawn in my comfortable bed of wet leaves under the van they got there and I went for my morning constitutional by the train yards. That trail there that you turn off of to go into the jungle, well, it, the trail, winds along all the way to the Grandview Cut, and then all the way out of town. Probably to New West, I don't know. Anyway, I'm strolling along minding my own business enjoying the day like you were just enjoying the sunshine on your face, then what do I happen to spy but a couple of dames up on the roof of the old Chenoweth Box Factory Building."

"There's nothing against the law about two dames being up on the roof of the Chenoweth Box Factory Building, so far as I know. Or any other box factory, even at dawn or thereabouts. Knowing you have an eye for a pretty lady, I imagine they were pretty ladies or they were ordinary ladies who were naked or something like that. Though I would have thought since you got hooked up with this little Ludmilla maybe your gaze wouldn't go awandering. Then, again, I remember your reaction to the Hungarian bombshell at the radio station."

"You know, Castle. I hate it when you talk like I write."

"Believe me, I'm sorry for that."

"Yeah, well. Enough of your bunkarino. I didn't know if the two ladies were pretty or not, at least I didn't that first morning, because they were too far away. But I looked again this morning."

"Were they closer this morning?"

"Yeah."

"Yeah?"

"Uh huh. Because this morning I had my binoculars. See, I slipped out of camp on the pretext of rounding up grub for the slumgullion and went to my apartment. I was back for the evening meal carrying a dozen large carrots, five pounds of potatoes, two pounds of round streak and, under my jacket, my Zeiss—made by the enemy—glasses. The bos loved me. Anyway, I should mention that the reason I was curious to get a close-up gander at the dames, is on account of what they were doing at dawn on the roof of the Chenoweth Box Factory."

"Which was?"

"One of them was lifting barbells and dumbbells, swinging Indian clubs, doing sitting up exercises and bending over to touch her toes."

"That is very interesting, Joe."

"You're being sarcastic?"

"No, I'm not. What was the other one doing?"

"She didn't seem to be doing much of anything. Just watching. Maybe she came over, helped the other get into her robe or something when they were done. Anyway it was all very intriguing."

"Yeah, I bet. All that bending over."

"No way. That kind of stuff never crossed my mind because I'm a pro. And being a pro, I returned to camp, got my binoculars. "

"And what did you see?"

"I saw that either one of them is very, very tall or the other one is very, very short. So I'm studying them and I figured if the one hoisting the barbells was merely tall for a woman, say five foot seven, then the other woman couldn't have been more than four foot seven. And that's kind of unlikely. Then I thought about your cabdriver the other day. You and Finnegan in the cab, the driver knew you from times past. He told you about the real tall woman with muscles he picked up at the train station. And I'm thinking about how if it was the same woman, it sure is a coincidence and ain't life strange. Then the tall one finishes up her health and culture exercises, and says something to the other one. And this woman goes to fetch a robe and bring it to her. Well I zoom in on the smaller one when she does this. See, before I was watching the big one and didn't really notice this one. So the first thing I notice as I'm adjusting is this shock of fire-coloured hair. Reminded me of the time last year when I found Cyril Fremont's body in the alley and opened the door to the garage and the flames shot out. Then I get a load of the face and, man, forget what I ever said about any other dame. This one was the end all and be all. I mean she wasn't just beautiful, she looked like she was ready at any moment to get down on the ground. I swear that was my first thought. Then, lo and behold…Well, what happens. She brings the robe and throws it over the other one's shoulder then she takes another step and they press up against each other and the little one stands on her toes and they kiss like Robert Taylor and Greer Garson in the movie Ludmilla and I saw the other night. *Waterloo Station,* at the Capitol. So, the next thing that happens is the big one pulls the little one's sweater over her head, starts making a meal of her breasts and then she, the big one, must have been thinking the same thing I had been thinking, I mean about the little one looking like she was ready to just get down on the floor, because the big one grabs her and pushes her down and they disappear from view."

"I think I'd like to get a close up look at that red head," Castle said.

"You want to fall by, use the binoculars?"

"No, I want to see her in person."

"Yeah, me too."

"But that might have to wait."

"What'd you mean?"

"We have other things to do. Tomorrow morning, you follow Fry Pan out of camp when he goes to the bus station for his meet. I'll be there hiding behind a potted plant, reading a newspaper, or something like that. Then I'll follow the other guy. If nothing turns up I'll be there in the afternoon to pick him up on Terminal Avenue."

"All right. I'll see you tomorrow. I got to leave now."

"Where you going, Joe?"

The reporter blushed.

"I get it," Castle said. "Ludmilla must live around here. You're going to stop in for a minute or two, eh?"

Frontenac touched the brim of his fedora and turned west on Nelson Street.

Castle was on the corner across the street from the bus station at ten minutes to eight in the morning, just looking over at the names of cities scrolled over the doors in neon tube letters. In spite of himself or his experience in these places, the names still held out the allure of adventure. New Orleans. New York. Boston. Seattle. Well, okay, maybe not Seattle. He had gotten off or boarded ships in all those places at one time or another. Back in 1925, he caught a ship in New York that took him to New Orleans and Belize City, where he picked up a coastal steamer to Nicaragua. Him and Red Batson, whatever happened to him? Last he'd heard Red was a foreign correspondant in China.

Ah, the bus station, cheek to jowl with the train station, heralding the coming and the going. There was a travel agent's office in the building, the plate glass window festooned with bright posters for ocean liner trips to the Orient. It had been a long time since he'd just taken off for the sheer hell of it. Lately, it was always a war or conflagration where the fate of freedom was at stake or seemed to be. He had to ask himself, and he did, if that wasn't just an excuse. Didn't he know by now that there was always a villain waiting to take over from another villain, and the second villain didn't care how many people had to perish to put him in place. In the beginning the second villain usually had you fooled, he dressed in his hero rags and said wonderful things and you went for it. Or you let yourself go for it.

Castle crossed the street and went into the station. There were rows of smooth wooden seats, metal lockers, boards that listed arrivals and departures, a news dealer, the travel agent and a soda fountain. He stopped for a minute before the travel agent's window, studied the picture of the CP Liner docked in Shanghai, lots of picturesque coolies in peaked hats, plenty of well-dressed white people waiting to greet their friends, one guy loitering at the bottom left of the poster, near a big open door, probably to a warehouse, very dapper, looking a lot like Warner Oland, trying to look local.

"May I help you sir?"

It was a slender man with thinning, curly hair, wearing a v-neck sweater over a white shirt and knit tie, coming out of the office. Castle was about to ask him if that was Warner Oland down there in the corner but then figured it would make the man suspicious and the man would be watching him while he was watching Fry Pan and Frontenac. He was about to admit to dreaming but figured the fellow could provide a good cover, so he said, "I was just wondering. How much to Shanghai?"

"Two hundred and forty-nine dollars, sir. That's return passage, of course."

"What about a stateroom?" Castle asked, glancing to his left and seeing Fry Pan come in.

"That would be two hundred and ninety-nine dollars, sir. Would you like to see our free brochure?"

"Why, yes. Yes, indeed."

The man turned and went into the office. Castle followed him a couple of steps, looked out the window and there was Frontenac lingering by the big doors, head doing the swivel. Castle reading his thoughts, 'Where the hell is that, Castle?'

He, meanwhile, was trying to plot Fry Pan's trajectory, eyeing the place for anyone who might be Greek or Italian or Portuguese.

The travel agent turned back to Castle and handed him a brochure.

"Our phone number is on the back, sir. Please call if you have any questions."

"Thank you, very much, indeed. I look forward to doing business with you."

"By all means."

Castle stepped out of the shop just as a voice was announcing, "Last call for Seattle. Bus leaving in one minute from gate three. Last call for Seattle. With stops in Blaine, Bellingham, Sedro Wooley."

Frontenac spotted him and backed out of the station. Castle watched Fry Pan cross the floor with his shuffle walk. Noticed a man under the departure boards, leaning with one shoulder against the lockers, reading the *Times*. Maybe he was reading Frontenac's column, and wouldn't that be droll? Noticed him there, in profile like that, because of his nose. It was large but slender and hooked. Reminded Castle of Danny Bartoli's nose. He remembered the first time he met Bartoli. The guy being embarrassed about his nose, Louise telling him it was an elegant one.

That was Fry Pan's man. The hobo approached him, pretended to be fooling with a locker. Castle read the guy's lips, him saying to Fry Pan, "Well?" But Fry Pan's head was turned away, Castle couldn't see his answer. They talked some more, then the guy took something out of his jacket pocket, a bill, folded the newspaper over it and handed it to Fry Pan who nodded and turned away.

The man frowned, seemed to be watching the hobo but Castle knew he wasn't. He was thinking, frowning.

Castle followed him out to the front of the station, staying well back, for fear the guy might have reason to know what he looked like. The man hailed a taxi and Castle hailed one.

"Follow that cab," Castle said, and the driver nodded silently, pushed down the flag and pulled into traffic. Castle had seen it so many times in the movies, had always wanted to do it himself but never'd had the opportunity. It had worked just fine, and he told himself he'd try it again some time, and was, therefore, sort of hoping, as the man's cab pulled up at the corner of Main and Hastings, that the guy would get out and Castle would get out, thrusting some money at the driver without looking at him, and he'd tail the guy who'd hail another hack, thinking to thrown off any tails, and Castle would have to wave down his own cab and he'd be able to say it to the next driver. But while he was thinking all this and half out of the cab, the man with the hooked nose scooted across Main Street and over to a car that was parked at the curb with the engine running and pointed south.

"Well I'll be damned," Castle said, opening the door.

"What was that, Bub?"

"Oh, nothing. Just talking out loud to myself. Hold on a second, eh?"

"Sure thing."

Castle might have figured he was past the point of being surprised in this life. Not that he would ever admit to being jaded; no, he'd explain that he was just accepting of whatever might transpire in this life. Having seen more than his share—and more than your share, too—what it took to ruffle his feathers was not so much what was transpiring across the street—two guys who looked enough alike to be brothers, having a talk—as what it signified.

The man who reminded Castle of Danny Bartoli, nodded his head and stepped away from the car. The guy who was Danny Bartoli shifted into first gear and pulled away from the curb.

Well, what the hell, Castle asked himself, and didn't have an answer.

"Where to now, bub?" the driver asked him.

"Hell if I know, pal."

Castle watched the man turn the corner and walk west on Hastings. He paid the driver, got all the way out of the cab and headed in the same direction with a vague notion of keeping on his tail. But when the man boarded a trolley car, Castle had to pin his hopes on the street, hope that it would provide some inspiration, that gutters might gleam with enlightenment, there'd be clues in cornices, that sleeping neon signs would wake to spell out the answer to all puzzles or that he'd stare longingly at upper windows and see letters applied by sign painters rearrange themselves into solutions.

Or, hell, since he was dreaming, maybe down the street at the Army-Navy Store, a three-story emporium of cheap goods where there was always a special sale, he could dig through the bins and find something with his name on it. But what did he know and what was he looking for?

He was looking for a twelve-year-old girl. She was the daughter of a radical anarchist adventurer turned international resistance leader. The girl was in this burg and the people who had her hoped Leandro would be lured out into the open where they could kill him. All right but they had to know where he was hiding which means they had a whole web of agents, including but not confined to a fake hobo, the winner of the Danny Bartoli look-alike contest and Danny Bartoli, the original. But, then, on the other hand, that was merely an assumption on his part. Perhaps Leandro didn't figure into this equation; perhaps Danny Bartoli was not a crooked cop, or a cop pursuing his fascist interests on the side. It could very well be that Bartoli was completely honest and after something completely crooked. For instance, maybe Fry Pan was a snitch in the pay of the police to be on the earie about some illegal shenanigans transpiring in the train yards. Maybe yard clerks or switchman were purloining war supplies from boxcars, something like that. The more Castle thought about it, the more it seemed reasonable. After all, if they wanted to remove Leandro, you'd think they'd just go in with guns ablazing. Unless, they were afraid of him. They should be afraid of him.

He didn't have an answer ready. The Manhattan Club was over the way. Maybe there were some answers there.

Ten o'clock in the morning, Art Sprague was standing like a statue behind the bar, a statue called 'The Publican.' Meaty hands pressed flat on the mahogany, starched white shirt, cuffs rolled up on thick hairy arms, black bow tie, a perfectly straight white line of scalp bisecting his plastered down black hair. He reminded Castle of pictures of John L. Sullivan in his prime. When Art took a step back from the bar, Castle noted his expanding belly and changed the mental snapshot to John L. of the Later Days.

"Top of the morning to you, Gene."

"Art. Whatta you know, whatta you say?'

"I say I know a gin and tonic was in here yesterday afternoon and she left a note for you. What'll it be?"

Castle liked to keep Art Sprague guessing. The owner of the Manhattan Club had an astounding memory. Years ago he had begun to test himself by remembering peoples' drinks. Later, it was as if the people became their drinks. Castle didn't want to be one of those.

"Bourbon rocks."

Art came back with the drink and the note. Castle took the folded piece of paper to a table by a window that would have looked down on Hastings Street if it hadn't been painted over. He took a sip of the bourbon and scoped the joint. There was only one other morning drinker, a man wearing a rug that was all askew. The man put the tip of his right index finger into his glass of whiskey, took it out and ran it over the top of his table. Stared like he was watching the water evaporate, then he did it again. Castle shrugged and opened the note, read: "That place? The Ronnie-man says it is located on the third floor of the old Chenoweth Box Factory but one must telephone first: Klondike 4-9798. Yours, Edith Wilton. P.S. Pray for me, Castle."

He drank up, stood and fought the temptation to sidle over and have a gander at the other man's art work. It was difficult but Castle made it to the door.

He hoofed it back to the Standard Building. Laura saw him, connected a line and told him she sort of hadn't minded seeing him in bed but was glad he was standing upright.

"Thanks, I think," Castle said. "Any messages?"

"Yeah, Louise phoned. She'll be in tonight. Hopes you'll be able to meet her at the bus station at nine-fifteen."

"Anything else?"

"Yep, one more."

Laura reached for a pink slip to hand him.

"Never mind that," Castle told her. "Just tell me what it says since I know you've read it anyway."

"A party named Fred Engels called. Wants you to get in touch with him."

148

"Thanks. And how're things with you?"

"Somebody calls me, hangs up the phone."

"You're a switchboard artist. Can't you trace the call?"

"The calls come in the middle of the night at home."

"Well it's good to know you're at home in the middle of the night."

"Thanks. Whoever it is never says anything so it's not even interesting."

"Probably some guy enthralled with you, Laura. Doesn't have the nerve to say anything. Just sits by the phone pining."

"I don't think that's what he's doing, pining."

"You heard from Danny boy?"

"No. Maybe it's him calling?"

"Maybe. Listen, did he ever mention having a brother?"

"He's Italian, right? Sicilian. They all have ten brothers and sisters."

"He ever mention any brothers in particular on this side of the pond?"

"I think he said he had two of them over here. Both kids, I think. Yeah, and there's another one, older than him I think just arrived a couple of weeks ago from the old country. Why?"

"Just wondered."

"Don't give me that shinola."

"No, I'll just give you the mysterious private eye expression."

"That's not what you ought to give me."

"Laura you're going to drive me crazy with that kind of talk."

"One of these days, Gene. I'm going to drive you crazy but not with talk."

"Laura."

"I'm sorry, Gene. From now on I'll watch my tongue. Whoops. Sorry. Wait, just one more thing."

"Yeah?"

"My time is coming."

"It is?"

"Yeah. I'm a woman. I know these things."

Castle shook his head in dismay, real dismay. What did she mean by it? Did she mean her time was coming in the sense of their time is coming? Their time together? Sounded rather presumptuous. How could she dare imagine that he would ever leave Louise?

He looked back when he reached the staircase, hoping to catch her concentrating on her plugs and wires, maybe read something in her face. But, no, Laura was staring at him. Her green eyes going right into him, as if she was reading something inside. Castle shook his head. Women.

Renny Weeks was in the hallway working with a dust mop. Castle hated to see him. He was almost a big handsome kid. Looked like a rugged young Billie Eckstine but with glazed eyes and a drooping lower lip.

"Hows'it, Renny?"

"Oh, I'm in tip top shape, Mister Castle. Ready to go ten rounds right now. Yes I am."

"Good, Renny."

"I'm ready for a rematch with Mendoza."

Renny Weeks dropped the mop and it clattered against the marble floor as he began to shuffle, hands up before his face. He shot out a jab, another one, followed it with a left hook, and a right.

"Combinations, Mister Castle. Combinations."

"Combinations, Renny. That's the ticket."

Castle wanted to run the remaining few feet to his office, get in there quick as he could and hide in a corner away from the sound of Renny Weeks' breath coming from his nose in snorts, from the sound of his slow shuffling feet.

But he didn't run. He played it very nonchalant. Until he reached his desk and the shelf over the radiator with the encyclopedia and the rum. He took down the bottle and volume fifteen, poured three fingers in a glass that could be cleaner, and knocked them back. He opened the encyclopedia to page six hundred and seventy-eight. He just couldn't get past that page and on to Molybendum. It wasn't Mollwitz that he seemed to be stuck with nor even the Molly Maguires. No, he kept going back to Moloch.

Castle sighed and settled back in his captain's chair and thought about Moloch. And about what Renny Weeks had said. Combinations, Mister Castle. Combinations.

CHAPTER ELEVEN

Castle in the Nash did two laps of Terminal Avenue between Main and the bridge, and was in the west bound lane when he saw Joe Frontenac with his bindle on his back come out of the jungle near the mattress factory. He pulled to the curb and honked the horn. Joe spotted him and crossed Terminal Avenue, got in the Nash.

"I'm getting tired of sleeping under the truck, Castle."

"It's good for you, Joe. Toughen you up."

"I want a nice soft mattress, soft pillow stuffed with pigeon feathers. This assignment's getting stale. No surprises since I saw the two women on top of the box factory."

"I know they call you Thrill-a-Minute-Frontenac so in order to satisfy you, so to speak, I got some thrills coming up."

"You do?"

"Yeah, but before I tell you about them, there's our old pal Fry Pan coming down the Avenue."

"Something's in the works, Gene. Fry Pan's been chatting up Leandro quite a bit these last couple of days. And Leandro, I got a feeling he's ready to bust out. He gave me a picture of his little girl. You got one?"

"Yeah. Beautiful kid. Spanish-colouring, fine English features."

"She's going to be a heartbreaker when she grows up."

"Let's hope she gets the chance."

"Yeah, Gene. See our boy over there by the service road. Looking up and down the avenue."

"Uh huh. Maybe he's watching out for this taxi cab that's slowing to a crawl."

"Must be. Yep. Now Fry Pan's approaching the cab like he recognizes whoever's going to emerge. And…there's our boy."

"You ever meet Danny Bartoli?"

"The cop? Koronicki's partner."

"Yeah."

"Briefly. When I went to the station house, ask a couple of questions about Professor Treherne. They catch the murderer?"

"No. They wouldn't extend much effort for an old Bo. So why'd you ask me about Bartoli?"

"This guy. You see a resemblance?"

"Well, I don't know. Kind of. Hard to tell with his hat on."

"I had a chance to give him a good look over earlier today. Except for the moustache, he could be his older brother."

"Maybe he is."

"Uh huh. If he is, he just got into town from sunny Sicily where maybe he palled around in Taormina with Il Duce."

"And now he's palling with Fry Pan. Wonder what the story is on him?"

"You ought to inquire with High-Line."

"I will."

"Those birds are up to no good, Joe."

"How do you know that?"

"'Cause they're walking up that service road and they're past the end of the mattress factory."

"I don't get it, Sherlock."

"It is several hundred yards beyond the parking lot and to the next place. They could have ridden the cab. But they didn't because they didn't want to leave a trail to wherever it is they're bound. Which means one of them, at least, is a professional."

"Where do you think that is, where there're bound?"

"Let's leave the comfort of my cozy short and find out."

They crossed Terminal Avenue and kept one to each side of the service road out of sight of the two men should the two men chance to look back. The road was gravel, humped along the centre, and wide enough for a big truck. Grass and weeds struggled up through the gravel, vetch was established at the borders. When they got to the far end of the mattress factory lot, Frontenac stepped out onto the service road, nodded for Castle to follow. The reporter pointed ahead and they saw the two men still walking beyond the next plant, a metal works shop, going full bore from the looks of it. You could see fires inside, hear metal hammering against metal, the hum and whirr of lathes and generators.

Fry Pan and the guy who looked Greek or Portuguese or like Danny Bartoli, turned toward the third factory. There was one building beyond this one and then a paved road.

"You know which building that is, eh Gene?"

"That's the place where a woman hoists barbells on the roof."

The two men climbed four concrete stairs to a loading dock and approached a door adjacent to the warehouse doors, sealed now with corrugated iron, newly painted a military green. The darker man took a key out of his pocket, opened the door and they went inside.

"Well what d'you think of that, Gene?"

"I'm trying to figure out whether our work just got easier or more difficult."

"How did it get easier, if it got easier?"

"I'll tell you after we go visit an old acquaintance of yours called Fred Engels."

"Engels? I don't know anybody called Fred Engels. What're you talking about? Aren't we going over there, try to get in the building?"

"What would we do if we got in?"

"You have a point."

"Let's go see Fred."

From Terminal Avenue to the Hotel Vancouver on Georgia Street only took eleven minutes in the cab, that time of day, but Frontenac must have asked Castle eleven times who this guy Fred Engels is. When they finally met, Frontenac hadn't any more clue who the man was than Castle'd had. Then, once they were over the fancy-that stage, Castle told them what he had in mind. They went over the plans for half an hour then Castle took his leave. He had to get the Nash and drive to the bus station and meet Louise.

He was looking forward to a quiet night trading stories and messing around back in the room at the Rose Hotel. He had a bottle of her favourite which happened also to be his favourite, as well as a big bouquet of flowers. Louise liked flowers. Driving to the bus station, his bad arm assisted by the inside of his knees, Castle had a vision of living with Louise in a comfortable cottage, one of those Southern California-style items over in Kitsilano, with a nice yard. Louise could have a garden with all the flowers she wanted. But, no, Louise was not the gardening type. The flowers she wanted were bouquets that men handed to her as they bowed or threw at her from the audience.

She looked drop-dead, drag-em-out gorgeous getting off that Pacific Coach Lines bus, right leg stepping down first, hem of her pleated, lightweight wool summer skirt riding up her right leg. Three soldiers standing near by, noticing, one nudging another with an elbow. Getta loada the dame. The dame being more than twice as old as any one of them. His dame. Her smiling when she saw him, smile changing to a look of concern. The soldiers giving him the once over, some guy with his right arm in the sleeve of his brown double-breasted suit, the jacket draped over his other arm that was in a sling. Maybe it was the half dozen obvious scars on his face or maybe it was the un-self-conscious, mess-with-me-at-your-peril expression—which camouflaged Castle's just as natural comic and ironic view of the world—or maybe it was both that made the soldiers look away.

"The hell happened to you, Gene?" Louise said after taking the flowers and kissing him.

"Got shot, Louise."

He noticed the same soldier nudge the same other soldier and both of them, as well as the third soldier, look at him closely.

"Not again."

"Yeah."

"How many times you been shot in your life, Gene?

"I don't know. Four or five is all."

"That counting the time in Georgia?"

"I never got shot in Georgia. Must have been some other boy friend of yours."

"Georgetown. I meant Georgetown."

"No, those guys missed but not by much."

"How much did they miss you by, Gene?"

"Missed me by about two layers of paint."

"That's close, Jack."

"Might be some more action tomorrow, Louise."

"Well I got back just in time. Poor boy. I go away and bad things happen to you. Let's go back and I'll do nice things for you. To you."

They kissed and, over his shoulder, Castle noticed the soldiers still looking. He gave them a big wink and walked away with his good arm around Louise.

Castle drove back to the parking garage off the alley between Hastings and Cordova, Louise helping him turn the wheel.

"How did you ever manage to drive to the station all by yourself?"

"Used my knees."

They were laughing and joking around until they got to the parking lot and put the Nash in its spot.

"This place always gives me the creeps," Louise said, getting out of the car.

The sound of their footsteps was amplified by the concrete. You expected gunmen to be hiding behind the rounded forms of automobiles, to be peaking around damp pillars. Maybe vampires slept in backseats.

Despite yourself, you listened intently for anything that broke the stillness. The wind blew a candy bar wrapper across the cement floor, and you imagined it was a thief dashing from car to car.

Louise breathed a sigh of relief when they were in the alley and their shoes crunching gravel. She talked about the troop shows. A stage set up in the middle of a field, some seats for officers, the rest of the soldiers sitting on the ground, the lights at night, waiting in the wings to go on, the applause before you even opened your mouth.

"Well, Louise, in your case that's not so surprising."

"Then you come out. They applaud and whistle but it dies down after a minute and you have to say something, do something. I'll tell you though, those boys make for a great audience. They want to squeeze every ounce of pleasure out of every moment because each one of them knows they may be going over the pond any day now."

They turned the corner onto Cordova Street and heard Deep South Durkins singing about his lost little girl.

"He's working late, isn't he?" Louise asked.

"Yeah, he usually packs up his guitar in the afternoon. 'Little girl, little girl. Where could you have gone?'"

"You thinking of changing careers, Gene?"

"I hear the thing twice a day, I got it memorized."

"He sure sounds sweet."

They glanced over at Durkins, and Castle waved. The man

nodded and began another song.

"Up ahead's the hotel, You looking for a little fun…"

"Hey, Gene. He could be singing about us."

"But watch your step, people…"

"What?" Louise exclaimed.

"Or you'll be looking down the barrel of a gun."

"Louise! Get down!"

Castle pushing her toward the curb and between two parked cars, going into a crouch himself and right behind her. The first bullet hit the rear fender of the first car, the second smashed the windshield of the car behind them. Mixed up with the sound of glass shattering was a woman's scream from the other side of the street.

"Nice homecoming you planned for me, Gene."

"Crack wise later, baby. Help me off with my suit jacket now."

Castle untied the knot at the nape of his neck and released the sling, noticing Louise folding his jacket neatly. Another bullet hit the pavement three feet away. Somebody hollering, "Call the cops, call the cops!"

Castle ventured a look through the windshield of the car in front.

"Where is he?"

"I'm not sure. But there has to be more than one. The bullets came too quickly. All I know is they're on this side of the street."

"You carrying?"

"Just the blade."

Two more shots. One broke the sideview mirror of the car

behind them.

"What do we do, honey?"

"They can't stand out there shooting for long," Castle said. "They'll either take off or make their move."

"Can we run?"

"I'm going to run."

"What about me?"

"You stay down, get under the car, if you can."

"Oh, thanks."

"It is a nice car. A La Salle. Like Mandrake the Magician drives. Hell, maybe it is his and it does tricks too. Make us disappear."

"Where you running to?"

"I'm running to them."

Castle got his throwing knife from the ankle holder, moved away from Louise and out into the street, keeping low and to the side of the La Salle. Peeking around the front of it, and not seeing any gunmen on the pavement, he scuttled the four feet to the next car. Someone was still shooting where they thought he was. After another car length, he heard a man's voice. "Time's up. Cops'll be here any minute."

"We didn't get him, I don't think."

"Come on, we scared him."

"That son-of-a-bitch, he don't scare."

You overestimate me, pal.

"Come on."

"You go. Bring the car up. I'm going down there."

"All right. Be careful."

Castle heard footsteps moving away and when he couldn't hear them anymore, hazarded a glance toward the pavement. He saw the man in the doorway of the Rose Hotel, in profile, holding the rod, hat pulled down to his eyebrows, pencil line moustache, the hawk nose. Castle looked down the street the way his partner had gone, then toward the cars where he and Louise had taken refuge. The man stepped out of the doorway and pressed his back against the wall of the building, took a few sideways steps, thought better of it and dashed across the pavement. He slipped between two cars, and edged out onto the street. He was two cars ahead, going the way Castle had just come.

Castle moved onto the pavement, slipped off his shoes and ran low in a crouch. He was one car away from Louise, at the front of the La Salle when the man stood up, pointed the gun downward, hollered, "This is it!"

Louise screamed and Castle jumped out, grabbed the man around the neck with his left arm, knife in the same hand.

"No, this isn't it. At least, not for me."

The man struggled to break free but Castle squeezed harder and when he couldn't squeeze hard any more, brought his right foot down on the back of the man's right knee. The man fell forward, his face smashing into the chrome hood ornament—the car was a Plymouth, the ornament the sharp prow of a ship; the gun went flying and blood spurted from his nose. Castle took a step forward and hit him hard in the back, down low and to one side, the side where the kidneys were. The man seemed to make a relaxed slide down along the grille of the Plymouth, over the bumper and onto the asphalt. He was still for a moment and then raised his head and cursed Castle in Italian. Castle put his foot, thinking it looked strange, his foot, in the black sock, on the back of the man's head and forced it back down, and the man was still again.

"Are you all right, Louise?"

"Yeah, baby. I was scared."

"It's okay now."

"One thing though, Gene. What took you so long? You stop for a drink?"

"Nothing was open."

They heard a siren.

"Here comes Koronicki."

"Yeah," Louise said. "This ought to be interesting."

"Yeah, especially when they turn the body over."

"What do you mean?"

"You'll see."

A few people started to close in on the scene.

"I saw the whole thing!" said a Japanese man.

"The cops'll want to hear," Castle told him, the man nodding eagerly.

The unmarked car came around the corner followed by the detectives' unmarked. The uniforms got out, glanced at the body and then looked up and down the street and even up into the air, as if trying to spy the crow who dropped a man in a suit between a Plymouth and a La Salle on Cordova Street. Koronocki and Bartoli came forward, walking between the shafts of light from the cruiser's headlamps.

"Well, well." Koronicki shook his head, brushed his hand down the front of his coat, as if he wanted everyone to think he was fastidious where crumbs and lint were concerned. "There's Gene Castle. And there's a body on the ground. Strange thing is the body doesn't belong to a dead person. I just saw a finger move."

Castle noticed that Koronicki's hair was now not much more than a memory.

Bartoli stared at the man on the ground. Castle saw him bite his lower lip.

"Who is he?"

"I don't know, Koronicki. Why don't you ask your partner?"

"Hell should I ask my partner?"

"He knows who it is."

"Danny?"

"I don't know what this scum is talking about, Chief."

"Scum is it? You know, Horace…"

"Don't call me that."

"You know, Koronicki. When I met him I thought it just dandy you had finally gotten a partner who resembled a human being. But this one's worse than the other ones, that shanty Irish and the more recent piece of Gorbels gutter trash."

"Why you son-of-a-bitch." Bartoli took a step toward Castle. "I'm going to tear your fuckin head off."

"You're going to have to be a better scrapper than your brother here. He had a gun and I have a bad arm and look where he is."

Koronicki stepped between the two men.

"What's this about his brother? Is that your brother?"

"Of course not."

"MacLachlan," Koronicki said to the closest guy in a uniform. "Turn him over and search him for identification."

The cop handed Koronicki the man's wallet. The man's nose was spread across his face and his eyes were almost closed but Castle was sure he saw the guy look up at Danny.

"That was real good, Danny. The way you didn't show any reaction at all except for clenching your teeth."

"That'll be enough from you, Castle," Koronicki said. "This says his name is Lawrence Griswold of 4231 Oak Street. I don't think Griswold is no Eye-talian name."

"It is not," Castle agreed. "But the guy curses in Italian which stands to reason on account of he's just arrived in this country two weeks ago from Sicily where he's a genuine henchman for the Fascist party. He's here to see his little brother Danny here who wants to be a genuine fascist."

"This has gone on long enough, Chief. Let me at him."

"Not now, Danny. Maybe later. You go help Olafson and Murphy talk to witnesses."

Bartoli gave Castle a parting look.

"Louise, Gene. You want to come down to the station house, give your statements?"

"No," Castle said. "I don't want to go down to the station house and I don't think Louise does either."

"Yeah. No fucking way."

"That's what I like about her, Koronicki. She's a girl who speaks her mind. We'll give you our statements right here."

"Gene met me at the bus station. We drove to the parking garage…"

"Where you going, Castle?" Koronicki interrupted her.

"I'm going to get my shoes."

CHAPTER TWELVE

"Well it is just like old times, ain't it?" said Castle, following Louise into a booth at Ramona's. Frontenac and Finnegan, a.k.a. Engels, sitting across the table.

But their faces were glum.

"Bad news?"

"Yeah," Finnegan nodded. "Bad news."

Finnegan looked at Louise.

"Louise knows everything that's gone on. Don't worry."

"Nice to see you again, Louise."

"And you, Mister Engels."

"You guys don't have to tell me what you said to get into the place," Castle said. "Or about any indiscretions on your parts. Just give me the scoop."

"Let me just say," Joe said, "that we ascertained that the red-haired girl we saw on the roof is the same one that was at Skinny O'Day's. Sanora, that's her name, appears to happy right where she is. She doesn't turn any tricks except with the owner of the place, the weightlifting broad."

"Did you get a close-up gander at that one?"

"Yeah. She's a, well, I don't know what she is, Gene. But she's one hell of a woman or one hell of a person. Six-five I'd say and she's got muscles on top of her muscles. She walked through this waiting room they have, classy-looking but kind of cold; the waiting room, I mean. I mean it has modern leather and metal chairs, metal sculptures. She came striding, or strutting through there a couple times, wearing a little tennis skirt—well, on her it looked little—white, high-heeled ankle boots like waitresses wear in restaurants in Budapest, and a sleeveless t-shirt. Quite a sight, let me tell you. Her legs go on forever and they have muscles I didn't know existed before. Same with her arms. I knew about biceps but she has muscles coming out of her elbows, it seems to me. Up top she looks even more unusual on account of, well, her chest reminds you of those anatomy drawings. Looks like she doesn't have flesh. It is all lines and sections. No breasts to speak of, just, you can see the nipples poking forward."

"Anything else about her?"

"Whatever else there is I don't want to think about. Oh, yeah. She's German."

"That's no surprise."

Frontenac looked at Finnegan who stared at his coffee cup. When neither spoke, Castle said, "Well that relieves me of one chore. I'll just tell Skinny the redhead doesn't want to go back."

"Yeah," said Frontenac.

"So you find out why the guy who looks like Bartoli went in there?"

"Yeah," said Frontenac. "Indeed we did."

"Well you going to tell me or what?"

Frontenac looked at Finnegan who just shook his head slowly.

"The girl's in there," Frontenac said. "Isabella. Martine's girl."

"That's what I figured. They keep her in a room? They going to ransom her? What? You find out anything?"

Finnegan sighed, when he raised his head there were tears in his eyes. He sniffed.

"Like you suggested, Gene, I telephoned from the hotel and told them I wanted, I, uh, wished to meet a young girl…"

"Oh, no," Louise exclaimed.

"No, no. Don't think that. I told them I was interested in meeting a young girl. We made an appointment. It was for fifteen minutes after Joe got there. I went into the room with the blonde. They told me she was thirteen but I knew the girl was at least fifteen. We went in the room and well, we didn't, I didn't do anything. All I did was ask her questions. She told me there was another girl there who really was young. Twelve years old. So after fifteen minutes, the blond left. There's an exit for the girls or boys or whatever they have and the clients. I talked to a man, this effeminate man, who works there, sort of like the secretary. I told him I wanted to meet a really young girl. The youngest one they had. And I wanted to meet her now. He said it was highly usual, booking an appointment like that. I said, they had a responsibility to me since they had taken my money under false pretenses, giving me an older girl. He disappeared to talk with the owner. Then he was back and he ushered me into her office. She has this big leather chair on a platform or dais. It's like a throne. When she gets out of the chair and moves around, she's like a panther slinking through the forest. She told me she had a special girl, twelve years old, really twelve. A beautiful girl who's only been out twice before. That's how she put it 'only been out twice.'"

"Oh, God," Louise moaned.

Maude appeared at the table holding her coffeepot.

"Refill?"

Nobody seemed to notice her and she left.

"Then what happened?" Castle asked.

"The woman told me it would cost. I told her money was no object. I paid her."

"How much?"

"Five hundred dollars."

"Go on."

"They sent me into a room. I gave it the once over for a hidden camera but I couldn't find one. If there was one they hid it well because the room was just as modern as the waiting room, the way Joe described it. No pictures on the walls. A raised bed, black satin sheets. But I don't know about a microphone and a recording device. There could have been one in the bed platform."

Finnegan stopped talking. He shoulders hunched and his body seemed to deflate.

Louise patted his hand. Finnegan breathed deeply.

"Take your time, Martin," Castle said, and brought a mickey of rye from inside his jacket.

"You never called me that before. It was always 'Finnegan.'"

Castle poured shots all around.

"Keep talking, Martin."

"So she came through the door, Isabella," Finnegan sipped. "She was terrified. Dressed like a Spanish schoolgirl in a pleated gray skirt, school jacket, white knee socks and black patent leather shoes. But she has this thick black hair and it was hanging loose. I don't know how anyone can do this to a little girl. She had on bright red lipstick and they had made up her eyes.

"I had my pad and pencil. I wrote 'Don't be afraid, Isabella. I didn't come to hurt you. I'm not going to touch you.' Then I put my finger up to my lips, wrote, 'I work for your father.' And she let out, an 'Oooh!' I was worried about that at first but then I figured if anyone were listening they would just think it was part of, well, you know. I wrote down that she shouldn't pay any attention to anything I say out loud just to what I write. I said, 'Sit on the bed…Lie back…You're a pretty little girl, aren't you.' Then I wrote that her father was close by and we wanted to come in to get her, 'Do they ever take you outside?' I wrote and handed her a pad and pencil of her own. 'No,' she wrote. I found out she had a room to herself but there were no windows and she wasn't able to let me know where in the building it was because she didn't have any sense of orientation, since they'd had brought her there blindfolded. She wrote that the big woman, the woman who kidnapped her, came to visit her at night. That's how she wrote it, 'comes to visit me at night.' The red-haired girl came to the room too but only with the big woman. The red-haired girl never touched her. The big woman wouldn't let her. She made her sit and watch. That's it. Give me some more of that whiskey."

Castle poured Finnegan another drink.

"Gene?" Louise said.

"Yeah, sweetheart?"

"You ought to kill that woman."

"I can't kill her except in self-defense."

"The things she's done."

"She's already done them. All I can hope to do is stop her from doing more."

"That poor little girl."

"It won't help the little girl, me spending the rest of my life in the joint."

"I'd like to get in there and kill the bitch."

"You'd like to get in there, eh?"

"Uh oh," Frontenac muttered. "Gene, you got that look."

"You're what, Louise. Five-eight, five-nine?"

"Five-eight."

"I know what you're thinking, Castle," Frontenac said. "There's no way. Louise can't do it. I've seen her be an old lady and a beautiful half-gypsy. But I've seen this lady too. Louise can't do this. The dame's too big."

"She's not going to try and pass as the dame. Just as a tall dame who's looking for another dame's who's big enough for her."

"Oh, no," said Louise.

"Oh, yeah, baby."

Eighty-thirty that evening, Gene Castle and Joe Frontenac got out of a taxi at Terminal Avenue and Clark Drive, walked west over the bridge and headed around the side of the mattress factory.

"I'm worried about this, Gene."

"It'll be fine, Joe. Well, maybe 'fine' isn't the word for what it'll be but the plan is in place. We've done what we can to be prepared."

"What about Louise? Her disguise? You sure it's the right one?"

"What the hell, she's a customer. What she's pretending to be, well, someone like that might dress any old kind of way. They don't wear signs."

"Yeah, but, well, she still looks feminine."

"What do you think she should do, dress as some sort of bull dyke? That would be too obvious. Also, the tariff is kind of high. She has to look like she can afford the rate. Nice tweed suit, conservative shoes. The haircut's a little hard to take but tomorrow, I'll buy her a wig."

"Tomorrow."

"Don't say it like that. Look, Joe, you just got stage fright."

"And what about Art Sprague?"

"What about him?"

"Can we count on him? I mean he got hurt last year on that caper down at Princess and Gore."

"Yeah, but he got us in there."

"I still don't think it's a good idea to take Leandro inside. He's liable to get too emotional. Start shooting if he doesn't see the girl right away."

"We need him. In addition to which he's the best. If he'd kept all the battle medals he's earned, he could dress up as the Christmas tree in the Hudson's Bay window."

They found the trail at the back of the loading area and followed it through the scrub of weeds and young alders to the edge of the train yards. Two hundred paces and they turned off to the jungle. They could hear the bos in there.

"Have your piece ready, Joe. He may be carrying."

"All right."

"Don't forget. Aim low."

"Yeah."

Castle trod heavily coming through the brush, kicking at salal and muttering nonsense to Joe. They heard High-Line talking, or reciting.

"Who's it coming, friend or foe? Well, looky here, it is Gene Castle and Deadline Joe. Only the latter's doffed his hobo threads. He's turned out like a citizen instead."

High-Line was in the middle of the clearing, standing by a fire, and the others were seated around him. Castle had the thought that High-Line stayed in the clearing all day, reciting. Fry Pan was there, Leandro, Laramie.

"What do you want, you and him?" High-Line asked. "The looks on your faces are determined and grim."

"We want him," Castle said, pointing at Fry Pan. The man sprang up from his milk crate seat and started to run, Martine made a grab for him and got hold of his arm. Fry Pan shook loose and took a swing at Martine, who blocked the swing with his left forearm, took hold of one of the man's ears with his right hand, twisted and put the man down on the ground on his stomach.

Martine held him there and Castle leaned over the man.

"How do we get in the box factory?"

"I don't know what you're talking about."

Castle took the knife out of its ankle sheath.

"I'm not going to play with you. Answer the question or I'll cut your ear off."

"You're crazy, I don't..."

Martine twisted the man's ear harder and he hollered, then Castle cut off the lobe of the ear and the holler turned into a scream.

Blood poured out of Fry Pan's ear and covered Martine's

hand.

"This is getting real messy, Fry Pan. Speak up."

"Oh, shit. It burns. I'm going to bleed to death."

"No, don't worry. I'll kill you before you bleed to death."

"You…you need a key."

"You have a key?"

Fry Pan didn't say anything.

"You just answered me, didn't you?" said Castle, who turned to Frontenac. "Search him."

Martine let go of Fry Pan's ear and when he did the man made a move to get up. Martine brought his shoe down on Fry Pan's achille's tendon, and once again the man yelled.

"Keep it up," Castle said, "and you're going to be a real mess before we're done with you."

"Nothing in his pockets," Frontenac said.

"Well, start taking the clothes off him. First the shirt."

Frontenac fumbled with the mother-of-pearl buttons on the shirt, then just ripped. The man had a belt across his chest, like a bandillero with pockets.

"You are not a pleasant sight, Fry Pan or whatever your name is. All that pale skin and ugly black hair."

"Quite a collection of passports, he has," Frontenac said. "Canadian, American and, hello, a German one. He's a party member."

"What party, Joe? The Grits? Tories? The CCF?"

"Why, no, Gene. The National Socialists. Here's his identity card: Josef Neuhaus. Joe Newhouse on this side of the water."

"What's your role in all this, Casanova?"

"*Scheisse!*"

"*Kannst eu an worten,*" Martine said.

The German muttered.

"What he say, Leandro?"

"He swears he will say no more."

"Oh, is that what he swears." Castle turned to Frontenac.

171

"Hand me the extra rod."

Frontenac took the gun from a shoulder holster.

"A Luger. How fitting." Castle handed the gun to Martine. "He won't talk so, obviously, he's no use to us. Shoot him."

Castle stepped back, Martine pointed the gun.

"I am with the—intelligence service—."

"How come the nearly perfect English?"

"My father was a diplomat. I was raised in London. Educated in Ottawa, in Boston. So naturally I was put to work in North America."

"Naturally. Who's the hook-nosed guy who, you may have noticed, didn't show up for your meets to today?"

"He's from Italy."

"I didn't ask you where he's from, I asked you who he is."

"Giovanni Bartoli."

"What's his brother got to do with this?"

"He recruited him. You people are so unprepared. So foolish. What do you think we in Germany have been doing since the miserable Treaty of Versailles? We have been preparing. For our revenge. It doesn't matter that I talk. Or that you kill me. The German machine, with some help from our fascist partners, is unstoppable."

"Nice speech. Since it doesn't matter if you talk—which is how you excuse to yourself that you don't have the guts to hold out—then you may as well tell us how many guns are inside the factory?"

"I will talk no more."

Castle turned his head toward Leandro, who shot the German in the wrist, shattering the bone.

"How many, did you say?" Castle hollered through the man's screams.

"*Vier! Vier!*"

"Yeah," Frontenac said. "You have a right to be afraid."

"No," Martine interjected. "*Vier* it means four. Four guns."

172

"We ought to go, Gene. Time's running out."

"All right, Joe." Turning to High-Line, Castle said: "Don't call the cops. Sorry, not that you would. Put a tourniquet on him, tie him up, and keep him quiet. I'll explain everything later."

"Whatever you say, Gene."

"What no rhyme?"

"I ought to quit if I can't find a rhyme for tourniquet."

"Later, High-Line."

"You fellows done real good," said Laramie Stribling. "Old Johnny Ringold couldn't of done better."

"Thanks, partner," Castle said.

"Say, Laramie?" Frontenac asked. "You ever meet Wyatt Earp?"

"Yep."

"What kind of fellow was he?"

The old-timer spat on the ground.

"That's what I think of Wyatt Earp."

"Were you at the gunfight at the O.K. Corral?" Frontenac asked.

"No, sir. I was in the hoosegow in Abilene but I got to Tombstone a couple weeks later. Gunfight, my ass."

"We'll be back later, Laramie," Castle said, "and you can tell us all about it."

He turned to High-Line.

"Can we get to those factories without going back the way we came?"

"Yes, my friend, follow the trail to the end. Make a turn to the right and go 'til the trail's out of sight. There is a path you can barely see, it'll lead you to the lee of the very last fac-tur-ee."

The trail petered out at a cement blockhouse used to store electrical gear for the railroad. They took the path to the right, following it through the bush to a muddy treeless slope that they climbed, finding themselves at the side of the Chenoweth Box Factory. All the windows in the redbrick wall were boarded up.

They walked slowly and quietly to the far end of the building. Castle looked at Frontenac. The reporter shrugged, spread his hands in a questioning gesture. Martine got down on his belly, crept forward and peered around the corner. He moved backwards, stood, and held up one finger. Then he touched Frontenac's revolver and his own chest.

Castle nodded. Martine made a gesture with his right hand like he was signalling an outfielder to play deeper. Castle nodded again and took his own look.

The man was halfway along the back wall, between them and the door they had watched Giovanni Bartoli unlock. There was a black '39 Cadillac right around the corner. He saw his own Nash near the door and the loading ramp, right where Castle had hoped Louise could park.

Castle bent down and in three strides was kneeling at the side of the Cadillac. He crooked his finger for Martine to follow, and opened his hand indicating that Frontenac stay where he was. Martine went to the car but barely paused, touching his own chest with his thumb. Castle nodded and Martine took off, staying low, keeping to the side of the building. When Martine reached the loading ramp, Castle thought he would keep to the ground but, instead, he stood, placed his palms on the top of the ramp, which came to the middle of his chest, and vaulted up with a movement worthy of the Olympics. In four strides, he was even with the lookout. Castle amazed that the man didn't hear him. But Castle heard Martine.

"Pssst!"

The man turned at the sound and Martine kicked him in the face. He barely made the ground before Martine was on him, his thumbs at the middle of the man's throat. Castle thought for a moment that he was going to hold the grip until the man stopped breathing but, no, Martine turned him over, pulled the man's suit jacket down, undid the man's belt and tied his arms in back of him. Then he took a revolver from the man's shoulder holster and a handkerchief from the man's pants pocket.

Martine stuffed the handkerchief in the guy's mouth and seemed about to put the revolver in his own waist band but he thought better of it and hit the man on the back of the head with the gun butt.

Castle stood and signaled to Frontenac.

He looked into the backseat of the Nash. Art Sprague was on the floor looking up at him. Castle nodded. While Sprague was getting out of the Nash, Castle put a hand on the hood. Louise must have arrived no more than five minutes earlier, right on schedule.

Frontenac and Art Sprague got to the door at the same time. Martine had never seen Sprague before, but just nodded at him, accepting him because Castle had picked him to be part of the plan.

Castle spotted a fire escape ladder at the corner of the building, to the left of the door. It was painted dark red, hardly distinguishable against the brick. He reached up but the bottom rung was just out of reach. Martine noticed, and Castle gestured for him to come over and give him a hand.

Martine pointed to himself, to Frontenac and Sprague and to the door. Castle nodded. Martine put his hands together, fingers entwined, and bent his knees, keeping his back straight. Castle touched his wounded left arm and shrugged, then put his foot in the saddle formed by Martine's hands, pressed down and vaulted up. He grabbed the bar with his right hand, and just long enough with his left to wince and raise himself, grabbing the next rung with his good hand. In a moment, he had his feet on the bottom rung, and looked down to indicate he was all right.

He saw Martine and Frontenac open the door and enter the building.

By the time Castle had climbed onto the roof, his left arm was aching. He couldn't massage it or it would hurt worse. After adjusting the gun at the small of his back, Castle brought the sling from his jacket pocket and put it around his neck, took the knife from its ankle sheath and put it under his forearm in the sling.

In the middle of the roof was a little shed that reminded him of an ice fishing hut. The shed had a tin-roofed canopy that protected barbells and dumbells and stacks of plates like metal pancakes.

He took a deep breath and opened the door of the shed. Castle counted ten steps down to the next level and was grateful they were iron and not wood so he wouldn't have to take his shoes off. He started down, hoping there was no one to see his feet and then his legs suddenly appear, somebody with a gun waiting to shoot when the rest of him showed.

There was no one. It was a large space, at least forty by forty feet, with three walls of exposed brick and a floor of wide wooden planks painted black. To the left was a door open a foot or so and Castle could make out the edge of a white porcelain sink. The far wall was a new addition, freshly plastered and with a red-painted door.

Diagonally, across from where he stood was another stairway leading down. Castle started toward it, walking slowly, carefully, and had gotten halfway when he heard a shot. A second later, the red door opened and Castle rushed toward the other door, the one that led to a washroom. He got behind it just before the woman came out.

She was the biggest woman Castle had ever seen, and she looked just as Frontenac and Finnegan had described her, six-feet-five with broad shoulders and narrow boyish hips. She was wearing high heels and a long satin robe that was open, revealing muscled legs and a stomach that reminded him of twin rows of rolling pins. Her chest was bare, he could see one long pointy nipple but no breasts. She wore a pair of white satin panties with something in them that made an irregular bulge. Her hands were big, one held a gun.

Castle waited until he heard her heels sound six times on the stairs. Then he made for the room that the woman had left. Inside, he saw Louise sitting on the bed. He knew it was Louise but he hardly recognized her.

"Well, you're fully dressed," he said, his voice hardly more than a whisper.

"A couple of minutes later and I wouldn't have been. This is a lady that likes her work, I can tell you. She only does other women, of course. And girls. How do I look?"

"Well to tell you the truth…"

Louise was wearing a tweed suit, skirt down to mid thigh, clunky shoes with thick soles and one-inch heels. No make-up.

"Christ, your hair is shorter than mine."

"If we get out of this, I'll be wearing a wig for the duration."

"Let's go down and join the party."

Louise took a small automatic from her handbag.

"She was doing a slow strip tease, said it would really get me in the mood."

"Did it?"

"It got me in a mood, all right, but not the one she thinks."

"Did you see, Isabella?"

"No, but the bitch, calls herself Hermione, promised me a real treat afterwards. A twelve-year-old girl. Said we could both have at her at the same time."

They left the room and went to the stairs. They could hear muffled voices from below. Castle whispered in Louise's ear, "Take off those sensible shoes."

There were ten steps down to a landing and they would be out of sight until they got there. After nine steps, Castle looked at Louise, shrugged and stepped down. He got a quick glimpse—Frontenac in a chair, Danny Bartoli standing at the side of the chair with a gun to Frontenac's head; another man in a short belted raincoat, cradling a sawed-off .22 rifle in his arms, the big woman shouting at Frontenac, in a high-pitched voice, German accent: "How did you get in?"—a quick glimpse before Bartoli saw him and fired.

Castle made an instantaneous decision not to retreat; instead he ducked and rolled down the stairs. By the time he hit bottom, the man in the raincoat was standing over him.

"Don't kill him, Amadeo," Danny Bartoli called. "He's mine."

Amadeo stepped back, rifle pointed down at Castle.

"Let him get up," Bartoli said.

Castle stood.

"Well, well. Daniello, Hermione, Amadeo. Looks like we have an international meeting of totalitarian interests."

"And who might you be?" asked the big woman in her incongruous, feminine voice.

"I might be Adolph's older brother but I'm not. And speaking of older brothers, Danny. How's yours? Pretty bad off, I hope."

"Yeah, Castle. He is bad off and that just means I'm going have more fun paying you back."

"Going to show me your stuff, are you?"

"Yeah, I'm going to show you what I've been holding back for a year now, Castle."

"Oh, Danny. You're going to show me in front of all these people? So that's how you're bent. No wonder it didn't work out with Laura."

Bartoli's face twisted into a grimace so full of hatred that it was almost comic.

Castle shook his head in mock disgust, looked at Frontenac, "He's so goddamn predictable, eh?"

"Take off your coat, Castle," Bartoli ordered. "Take your arm out of that sling."

"Sure, Danny. How about my pants? You want me to take them off too."

Castle heard the big woman laugh in back of him.

"You men," she said. "Yes, predictable that's what you are. Both of you. All of you."

Hers was an international look of condescension.

"After you beat him," she said to Bartoli, "kill him. And the little man, too."

178

With that she strode across the room, long legs flashing in the opened robe, a bulge in her underwear. She is rather stunning, Castle thought, in her particular way.

He removed the jacket, and laid the sling with the knife in it carefully on the floor. He wondered where Louise was, where Martine was.

Bartoli stood between Frontenac's chair and a table. He put the gun on the table, took off his jacket and put in on the table on top of the gun, and stepped toward Castle.

"Let him go, Amadeo. Come on Castle, get your fists up. Like she said, I'm going to beat you before I kill you."

"Gee, you're a hard man, Danny. Fight a guy with a bad arm."

Bartoli moved to the centre of the floor, began sliding to his right, then to his left. He was a left hander which meant his right foot was forward, his right fist out front, left up by his left shoulder. Castle moved to his right when Bartoli moved left, then Castle feinted. Bartoli lead with his left, Castle slipped it and caught Bartoli flush on the point of the chin with his own right.

Bartoli leaned back and went down. He didn't collapse, just hit the floor like he was a tree and Castle the guy with the axe.

Castle shook his head slowly, not believing it had been so easy. But before he could take any pride in his work, he heard the word "Basta!"

And turned to see the .22 levelled at him.

"Enough!" the guy, Amadeo said, as if he just remembered the English word.

"Now I kill you."

There was a shot but it didn't come from the Italian. Louise was there on the landing with her little automatic, and she fired again. Both shots missed but Amadeo had turned to her, was just about to fire, when Castle tackled him. The guy held on to the rifle though, held on even after Castle had hit him twice in the face, but he dropped it when Frontenac kicked him in the head.

"Sorry I missed," Louise said, coming the rest of the way down the stairs.

"You did the job," Castle told her, and saw Frontenac turn his attention from the guy on the floor to Louise.

"What's the matter, Joe? You want my autograph, you think I'm Marie Dressler?"

Frontenac picked up the .22.

"Even though I saw you before, I still can't reckon it."

"Save it for the Style section of your rag, Joe. We got work to do."

Castle led them to the stairs.

"Where's Art?" Louise asked. "Where's Leandro Martine?"

Frontenac shrugged, "I hope they're downstairs. I hope they're okay."

"Well, we're about to find out. Louise you go first."

"Why me?"

"Cause you're the woman who's missing her woman."

"Yeah."

Louise closed her eyes—Castle saw the muscle twitch along her jaw—then she opened them and took the first step. Halfway down the stairs, she called out, "Sweetheart? Where are you, baby?"

A few seconds later, Castle and Frontenac heard another voice.

"Yes, what is it? What was all the shooting about? There were intruders. Was it them?"

It was a male voice, and just barely.

Frontenac whispered to Castle, "That's the secretary. The fellow we told you about."

"They're taken care of, don't worry."

"And who are you?"

"Me? I was with Hermione and…"

"Oh, yes. Hermione had to check on something in the back. She'll be reunited with you soon, I'm sure. I know what it's like to be interrupted."

180

"Thank you so much."

"Why not at all, darling. Hermione has taken quite a fancy to you."

"Oh, how do you know that?"

"She told me, darling."

"Splendid. And what is your name?"

"Lester. Pleased to meet you."

"Same here. Well, Lester, the thing is, I've taken quite a fancy to her too and I'd like to have her back. Now if you could…"

"Certainly."

The next thing they heard was Lester calling, "Dietrich! Dietrich, come here please."

Footsteps, then "Yes?" A deep voice.

"Dietrich, please go to Hermione and tell her her cli…her friend is waiting."

Footsteps going away.

"I love him wearing the hat indoors, it's so sexy. He's gorgeous, don't you think?"

"I suppose," Louise said. "If that's what one prefers."

"This one does."

They both could be heard laughing, then Louise saying, "Lester, we're both alone, eh?"

"Yyyeah…"

Lester tentative, drawing it out.

"Since we are, I got something for you."

"You do?"

"Yeah."

Then they heard the unmistakable sound of bone hitting bone, and a body falling to the floor.

Frontenac looked at Castle, "What the hell?"

They hurried down the stairs and saw Louise standing over the pretty boy and rubbing the knuckles of her right hand. The kid was out cold, lying there on his back in white duck pants and white v-neck sweater, blond hair parted down the middle.

Louise shrugged, "Had to stay in character."

"Yeah," said Castle. "But he looks so delicate."

"Maybe but I'm shorter than he is."

"Since you did so well you can lead Joe down the hallway where Dietrich went. What does he look like?"

"Dietrich? Medium height, brown camel hair coat, brown fedora."

"That's where I was the other day," Frontenac said. "Two rooms each side, another at the end."

"Fry Pan said there were four guns inside. Counting Dietrich and Amadeo but not counting Danny, we've only seen two."

"That's right. So we should be in for a couple of surprises."

"You go with her, Joe."

"Scaredy cat," Louise said.

They went off, got a few yards down the long hallway before a door opened and Castle ducked back into the foyer. He saw the guy in a brown jacket appear.

"Hey, Dietrich," Louise said. "Lester sent me down here on my own."

"Yeah? Who's the squirt in back of you?"

"I don't know. Lester told him something about a redhead."

"Yeah," Frontenac said. "The redhead. But he didn't tell me which room. He seems to be in kind of daydream or something."

Louise stepped around Dietrich and kept walking.

"That sissy-boy. He's crazy," Dietrich said. "Sanora don't do turns, he knows that. Must be on the pipe again."

"That's all well and good," Frontenac said. "But where does that leave me?"

"That leaves you waiting in the hall until I come back."

"But I paid good money, and a lot of it."

"Just shut up and wait."

Castle heard footsteps coming and ducked out of sight behind the heavy armchair where Frontenac had been sitting.

The guy walked past him, took a look at Lester on the floor and kept walking. Smart man, Castle thought, maybe he's headed back to the Fatherland.

Castle saw Frontenac standing in the hallway when a door opened and Art Sprague motioned him and Louise inside.

"Gene!" Frontenac turned and called to him.

Inside the room, they saw a short, fat and naked man face down on a wooden platform, his wrists and ankles fastened to metal poles. Castle noticed the wedding ring on his left hand. Seated on a leather divan near the head of the platform were two boys who looked to be about fifteen or sixteen, one a native Indian, the other white, both of them wearing nothing but athletic supporters.

"These rooms are pretty much sound-proof," Art said, and nodded toward the bed. "For obvious reasons."

The man on the platform had his bald head turned to the right.

"Is this part of my session?" he asked.

He twisted it further, until he could see Frontenac.

"How about you, handsome? The more the merrier."

Frontenac turned away and the man sniggered.

"Somebody throw a towel over his ass," Castle said. The white kid giggled.

"This guy means it. He can't get enough. We take turns with him. Jesse did him three times and I was on my third when John L. Sullivan there, walked in. I thought he might have paid to watch so I just kept at it. But he made me stop and…"

"You don't have to tell us any more, kid."

"Wait'll Koronicki gets a load of this," Frontenac said.

"Who's Koronicki?" the white kid asked.

"A cop."

"Oh, no," said the white kid. "My mother'll kill me!"

"That's nothing compared to what your fat boyfriend's wife will do to him," Castle said.

"Let us out of here, mister."

"Okay, get dressed. Art, lead them out. Frontenac, go up with him. You guys can bring Bartoli down, he should be waking up soon. Then we'll make our move."

The boys didn't have to be hurried. They were soon into their clothes, Art Sprague rushing them toward the door.

"We're not queer, you know," the white boy said to Castle.

"I know. You're just a couple of lads working your way through normal school."

Both boys were giggling as Art lead them away.

A few minutes later, Art and Frontenac were back carrying Danny Bartoli.

"He's still out," Castle said. "I'm surprised."

"You hit him good, Gene, but not that good," Frontenac said. "Danny got kind of ornery when we woke him up, so Art had to add one. "

"Drop him on the platform and shackle him."

"Should we let the good citizen go?" Art said. "I've seen him in the Club a couple of times. He's a dubonnet rocks."

"Figures," Castle said. "No, he looks like trouble."

"That's my middle name," the bald man said. "Hey, take the towel away. If you look at my sweet pink rear again, you might change your mind."

"Art," Castle said, "You see the other guy, Dietrich, anywhere?"

"Not a sign," Art said. "Must have got out while the getting was good."

A couple of minutes later, they were ready to go.

"Look at them there together, tied up like that," Frontenac said. "They make a fine couple."

"Yeah," Louise said. "Who knows what they'll get up to when we're gone."

"Uncover my ass!"

Castle stayed in the opened doorway of the room and watched the others walk down the hall, to the door at the end, Louise going first, Art and Frontenac a couple of steps behind and to each side of her. The men got out of the way when Louise knocked on the door.

It was opened by a man who was about Frontenac's height but his complexion was a lot worse. In fact, other than size, the two had nothing in common. It wasn't just that this man was ugly and that muscles bunched under the fabric of his suit jacket. No, you looked at him, and you saw a stone killer. It might as well have been written on his face.

Castle had to fight the impulse to leap out and shout for Louise and the other two to be careful. But that wouldn't do any good.

"Yes, what is it?"

He was in a sort of antechamber or vestibule. Castle could just make out the sliver of a door behind him.

"Hermione," Louise said. "She left me. I want what I paid for."

Castle expected the man to take out his piece, threaten to shoot her but instead he said, "Just a minute"—and closed the door.

They all seemed to be frozen in place for the time until he returned. Louise facing the door, Frontenac, his back against the wall to the left of the door, Art Sprague in the same position on the other side.

The door opened and the little man, appeared, a revolver in his right hand, the arm down at his size, a thick white envelope in the other.

"Madame, is very sorry but she has been detained by an urgent matter. Here is your five hundred dollars back and a little something else in addition. She hopes you will make another appointment at a later date."

"Yeah, fat chance of that," Louise said. "What am I going to do in the mean time?"

"That is not my…"

Frontenac stepped away from the wall before he could finish the sentence. The man turned, his gun hand lifting from his side. Art Sprague hammered him on the back of the neck with the side of his closed fist. The gun went off as the man went down. Frontenac fell over him.

"Oh, no!" Louise cried.

Sprague kicked the little man in the head and kicked him again for insurance.

Castle stepped out of the doorway to rush to Frontenac but before he got two steps the reporter struggled to his feet.

"You hit?" Castle called.

"No, I just tripped."

"For chrissakes. I mean, good. Now you and Louise stay out of the way but keep your hands filled. That other guy might have heard the shots and come back. Art and I are going in."

Art was waiting for him in the vestibule. When Castle got there, he nodded and Art opened the door. There was nobody to shoot, just a twenty by twenty foot room with a black-and-white-tiled floor, a skylight, velvet drapes covering part of one wall and a life-sized bronze sculpture of a muscular woman in a loin cloth making like the man on the Arm-and-Hammer box. Castle looked at the loincloth that seemed to be stuffed with bronze socks.

"Our hostess, evidently."

Art nodded his head toward the drapes and Castle nodded back.

They went over. Castle tugged at the rope, the drapes drew back quietly and Art opened the door.

It reminded Castle of one of those scenes on the other side of velvet ropes some place the teacher took the class in the afternoon to give them a glimpse at other cultures. A typical pioneer tableau from a cabin in the Canadian north or an eskimo family in their igloo having a nice dinner of raw fish, rubbing noses, that kind of thing. But this was a diorama from a much stranger museum.

The bed was nearly as big as Castle and Louise's entire room at the Rose Hotel. It was covered with satin sheets and big satin pillows and on it the giant of a woman was cradling Isabella who was made up to be a big girl such as you might find in another kind of brothel, one that catered to relatively normal men with relatively normal tastes. On a chair to the left of the bed, his back to the bed, reading a magazine called *Health and Physique,* was a man Castle had seen before. He was the sort of fellow you didn't easily forget. When he'd first seen him, ten months earlier, Castle had suddenly been afraid that his was the last image he'd have in this life. He was about as big a man as you'd ever encounter outside of a sideshow, and that was only part of it. On a sofa on the other side of the bed was the red-haired Rossetti girl, her skirt most of the way up her thighs—her legs were bare and lightly dusted with freckles—her hand was all the way up her thighs, her head against the back of the sofa, her eyes looking at the ceiling.

One pair of eyes looking at the ceiling, one pair fixed on a magazine with photographs of muscle men not half as muscular as the reader, one pair looking at the top of a little girl's head, the little girl's eyes blankly fixed on a woman's chest with no breasts only nipples that stood out like slugs.

Someone appeared at Castle's side. He had a moustache. He was wearing a brown camel-haired coat and a hat. Castle had the thought that he should go for his knife or gun but as soon as he had the thought, it simultaneously occurred to him that he would be too late. Then the man touched his arm and he recognized Leandro Martine. Castle started to move but Martine held him back.

Art Sprague stepped into the room and the woman flung the little girl aside, the red-haired girl stopped looking at the ceiling and took her hand from under her dress. The man in the chair turned his head and Castle saw a face that Melville might have been describing instead of that of Queequog, calling it "a crucifixion to behold."

The tableau came to life.

As the giant was in the act of standing, Castle had the notion that he would keep going, his head busting through the ceiling.

Castle took a step into the room.

"So Axel, I see you're still wearing the white makeup and painting your eyelids. Oh, sorry, I just remembered you don't speak English."

"I now speak some," said the big man. The left side of his face was covered with one inch scars as if someone—it would have been a group of someone's—had held him down and carved him up. The other side of his face had been smooth until ten months earlier when it acquired it's lone scar, a long one courtesy of a broken whiskey bottle wielded by an old Wobby friend of Castle's named Frank Wheeler.

"In six months of prison, I learn many English words."

"Let me have him, Gene," Art said. "I owe him one."

"No, Art, stay back."

"My back still hurts from when he hit me."

Axel laughed.

"And, so, what makes you think this time it would be different?"

The big woman got off the bed and took a step.

She was still in her robe and panties.

"Stop right there or I'll shoot you," Art said.

"No, you will not shoot my sister," Axel said, as if talking calmly to a child who wanted to leave the house without his mittens.

"Big strong man," Hermione taunted. "Why don't you put down the gun. Let's duke it out."

"Well, Axel," Castle said. "That's quite a sister you have. She really is your sister, eh?"

"Yes, that's right. My older sister."

"Runs in the family, eh?"

"Except for my brother Ludwig in the SS. He's only six feet high."

"If you win," Hermione talking to Art Sprague, "you get the

girl."

"What do you get, if you win?"

"Just the satisfaction of putting another man in his place. On the floor at my feet where he belongs."

Castle wanted to tell him not to do it but there was no point.

"All right. You act like a man, let's see if you can fight like one."

The woman smiled a wide condescending smile. Her teeth were yellow.

Art Sprague bobbed and weaved but the woman just stood motionless. She turned her head away and said something in German to her brother, and both of them smiled.

Art swung at her before she turned back but she was able to shift, just a bit so that the punch struck her a glancing blow high up on the side of her head. She hardly seemed to flinch. She laughed.

"You don't have much but do try again."

Art swung and missed. The woman didn't even have her hands up. "I bet you really want to fuck me, don't you?" she said. "Well you don't have enough in your pants."

"What I got is real," Art said.

Castle shook his head.

"Here, I'll show you what's real."

The woman started to throw, pulled her punch but Art had committed himself with his right. The woman ducked it and was suddenly in back of Art, one arm around his right arm, her other arm under his left. Art struggled futilely. She tripped him and got on top of him, jammed her thumbs into his eyes. Then she held his arms down and began to move her bottom back and forth on his stomach.

"You like that? Is that what you want?"

Then she laughed and got off him.

"It seems as if I get to keep the girl and also get the satisfaction."

Art sprang to his feet and made a rush at the woman, who pivoted, moving her body and her right leg to the right but keeping her left foot planted on the floor. Art tripped over her leg and went sprawling toward Axel.

"Oh, so you have come once more to me."

"Maybe he wants you to fuck him," Hermione walked back toward the bed.

"Perhaps," Axel said. "But I find him not attractive. Him I will kill, not fuck."

Axel lifted Art Sprague from the floor, Castle remembering how the man had done something similar last year, lifted him like a sack of potatoes, and Art had gone about two-twenty-five back then. He was bigger now. He grabbed the back of Art's collar, the bartender's struggles seeming irrelevant.

"So it was your back I hurt, yes?"

And Axel sent his big fist into Art's lower back. Sprague collapsed on the ground.

"That's enough," Castle said.

"Yes? And what do you intend to do?" Axel asked. "You have no gun. Your arm is in a sling."

Castle took the knife from its hiding place in the sling, drew his arm back and brought it forward, underhand, blade down, wrist stiff until it was perpendicular to the floor, and he let go. The knife seemed to whisper its way across the room and found its place in Axel's stomach.

"No, no!" Hermione screamed.

Axel swayed and stared at the handle of the knife. His right hand moved toward the handle, but before he could grab it, the big man fell forward and the end of the handle hit the floor first.

Castle looked from the man to his sister, in time to see her take the small automatic pistol from inside her panties.

"I kill you for this," and she fired.

It happened too fast for Castle to either be scared or to reach for his own gun. His first reaction was one of relief that she had evidently missed.

With her left hand the woman grabbed the girl by her thick black hair and pulled her close, then she shifted her grip and held the girl in front of her chest. Castle had his own gun out by then.

"I do not think you will try to kill me, Mister Castle. That's who you are, is it not?"

"Yeah, that's me."

"But I will kill you, if necessary. It really isn't necessary though. Now, let your gun fall to the floor."

Castle did as he was told.

She laughed.

"It is not necessary for me to kill you because I have servants for that."

"Dietrich!" she called. "Dietrich, *komm her.*"

"Yabohl, mien…"

He walked into the room then and the woman commanded him, "Dietrich take his man and…You…You are not, Dietrich."

The woman pressed the girl tighter to her chest. Castle saw Isabella's eyes come alive for the first time.

"Martine! It is you. Put that gun down and all will be well."

"All your people are dead, Hermione," Castle said. "You don't have a chance now."

"Oh, I do not?"

Then, speaking to Martine, she said: "Put down the gun. What can you do? Try and shoot me. Go ahead, you'll shoot the girl."

Martine didn't speak, just raised the gun.

"You wouldn't dare. She's my girl now. I'd hate to loose her but I'd find another one."

She threw her head back and laughed, a big laugh full of yellow teeth and that's the last living image of her that Castle would ever have because Martine fired and the bulled hit her in the mouth. The lower part of her face exploded, ejaculating blood and yellow teeth.

She seemed to stare at Martine with the eyes that were all of her face that remained intact. Isabella slid from her arms and the gun dropped to the floor.

Martine broke the stare by firing again, hitting her in the left eye. She pitched forward onto the floor while the redhead screamed.

Martine fired again, this time firing at the crown of the big woman's head, bursting her skull apart.

Isabella ran to her father and put her arms around his waist. In her patent leather heels, she came up to his chest.

The red-haired girl got off the couch and fell to the floor on her knees beside Hermione. Then she lay down and embraced the dead woman, lifted her head and kissed what remained of lips in her broken bloody face.

Martine took his daughter out of the room.

Frontenac came into the room and went to get a closer look at the red-haired girl and the dead woman. He took out his notebook and pencil and began to write.

"We better see to Art," Castle said.

"I'll take care of him," Louise replied.

She went into the washroom and came back with a towel soaked in warm water. She knelt beside Art and placed the towel over his eyes. Castle watched and saw Frontenac watching her. Frontenac looked at Castle and looked away.

Martine returned with Isabella. The makeup had been washed from her face but she was still dressed in trollop's clothes.

"We're going to have to call the police soon, Leandro. So you and your daughter better vanish."

Martine nodded.

Castle took his car keys out of his pocket and tossed him at the soldier of fortune.

"It's the Nash out by the loading ramp. It isn't much but it'll get you out of town."

"But how are we going to explain all this?" Frontenac asked.

"There's a Mister Engels at the Hotel Vancouver who will explain everything," Castle said.

"I won't say that I am in your debt, Mister Gene Castle. That I am in debt to all of you."

"No, don't say it, Mister Leandro Martine. I wouldn't like to think of you labouring under such a burden."

"It would be an honour to fight beside you again. Come to Europe and help me."

Louise looked up from where she was kneeling beside Art.

"If I did…" Castle started to reply.

"Oh, no," Louise said.

"How would I find you?"

"Maybe I'll be in France, maybe I'll be in Spain. In Norway. Who knows? There is a lot of work to be done. You know the kind of people to ask to locate me."

"Yeah, I do."

Martine went to Art Sprague, got down on one knee and put his hand on the bartender's chest. "Anything you want, my friend. I won't forget."

Then he started to shake hands with Louise but Louise kissed him on the lips. Castle would have sworn he blushed.

Martine embraced Frontenac, nodded at Castle and was gone.

They stared at the swaying velvet drapes.

"Who the hell is that guy?" Frontenac wondered out loud. "And what's going to happen to him?"

"A man like that," Louise said, "I wouldn't worry about him. It's the poor little girl I worry about. I'll worry about her as long as I live."

"Poor Isabella," Castle said.

"What do we do now?" Frontenac asked, still looking toward the drapes.

"We call Koronicki. I can't wait to see the expression on his face when he gets a look at his partner."

EPILOGUE

It was two weeks later in Ramona's Café. There was a private party going on in the back booths. A few bottles could be seen making the rounds.

"Little girl, little girl..."

Harry 'the Hipster' Heinz was sitting with his legs crossed, cuffs of his slacks half-way up alabaster calves, little C-Melody saxophone balanced on a bony knee while he offered little four-bar embellishments to the blues that Deep South Durkins was picking on his guitar. Raymond Thomas, inspired by the sight of another Negro, had abandoned his usual seat at the counter to join the party. His friend, Guy Roberts, accompanied him. The millionaire tycoon had pulled up a chair next to the rhyming bindle stiff, High-Line Mason. Frederick Engels was there at a booth with Joe Frontenac, the bookie, Beanie Brown and his friend, a Japanese guy whom Beanie had described earlier as a serious punter. The Japanese fellow, his hair greased back on the sides and with a high pompadour in front, didn't seem to know what was going on but was decent enough to laugh every few minutes. A Ramona's sort of guy, Castle thought.

"Here we are cutting up touches, a motley group such as"—High-Line holding up one pudgy finger—"you're not likely to find too many other places down the line."

Everyone laughed, and High-Line took the bottle of rum passed to him by Deep South Durkins.

"Aw, shucks, ain't we coo-zy. If I have anymore of this it might make we woozy." Mason drank anyway. "Now that rhyme was a doozey."

"Well, there, Gene," Raymond spoke. "From what I heard that was some jackpot you all got yourself into."

"True enough, Raymond. Too bad you missed it."

"No, it ain't."

"He didn't walk without crutches for six months," Guy Roberts said.

For a couple of moments no one said a word. They were caught off guard because Guy Roberts had spoken, actually said something to them. Roberts saw the expressions on their faces, and looked embarrassed.

Louise, in a blonde wig, took the bottle and let the neck hover over the tycoon's glass.

"A refill, Mister Roberts?"

"Why… Guy. You can call me Guy."

"Refill, Guy?"

"Yes, ma'am."

"You can call me Louise."

"Yes, Louise."

Louise filled the tycoon's glass. Castle saw Laura looking at him. Her eyes shifted to Louise and Guy Roberts. Then they returned to him, and she raised one eyebrow.

Castle shook his head just slightly telling her she was crazy.

"Meeting them women, drinking that rum."

Deep South starting to improvise. High-Line adding, "Always scheming, just an irresponsible son of a gun."

The Hipster getting spunky with the melody.

Deep South took his hand from the belly of the guitar and reached for his drink. "That one might amount to something, we work on it."

"Mister Durkins?"

The black man looked up, saw Frontenac leaning over the back of the booth.

"Ain't nobody ever call me Mister Durkins before," he said. "I don't know whether I like it or not."

"Okay, then. Deep South. I'd sure like to do a story on you. Newspaper story."

"Newspaper story? Why, son, you flatter me."

"What about me?" the sax man interjected. "You're looking for some material, how about 'The True Story of Henry the Hipster.'"

"He prints the truth about you," Castle said, "you'll be in the joint before the bundle falls off the truck."

"Yeah, daddy. I see your point."

"Speaking of stories," Frontenac said. "Laramie, when I was in the jungle with Castle, you were talking about Wyatt Earp. Said you'd tell us about him."

"Why that Wyatt Earp," Laramie Stribling shook his head. "He certainly was no friend of mine."

"Wyatt Earp," sang Deep South, "He weren't no friend of mine."

"Just a cheap piece of trash."

"Cheap piece of trash blowing along the gutter," Deep South sang.

"A cheap piece of trash, a punk you'd like to thrash," intoned High-Line, not to be undone. "He belonged in the gutter, him and each and every brother, too evil to be born of a mother."

"Now let me get on with my story," Laramie said. "Like I told you boys: By the time I got to Tombstone, the Earps had gotten off on account of a rigged jury. One Clanton had been murdered and one McLaury. Now old man Clanton, name of

196

Newman told me…"

Just then the door of Ramona's opened with a clatter and a guy with bloodshot eyes who needed a shave came in. He was wearing a cab driver's hat and glancing around the café. When he glanced over at their booth, Castle recognized him and he recognized Castle. It was the guy who'd driven him and Finnegan around, same guy Castle had met years ago and had taken him and Louise and Frontenac to the docks when they sailed to Europe.

The cab driver came over and handed a large brown envelope to Castle.

"This was waiting for me when I came on shift today. How does anyone know I ever met you? I can't figure that out. Unless it is from that guy there who dresses like he comes from Toronto, I think, which is where I came from which I told you one time—Cabbagetown—but I don't figure you to remember that. Only it can't be that guy on account of why wouldn't he give it to you personally being as how he's sitting right next to you?"

"Yeah, yeah. I remember you knew Hughie Garner and you were stuck in a refridgerator car somewhere in Saskatchewan. Maybe some time you can tell me."

"Maybe the next time I drive you to the docks to take a ship somewhere. But a guy like me I have to stay where I am and work day in and day out, and…"

"Are you going to give me the envelope or not?"

"Oh, yeah."

He handed the envelope to Castle.

"What's the second thing?"

"Louis over Godoy. TKO in the eighth."

Beanie Brown looked at the Japanese guy and the Japanese guy reached inside his pocket for his billfold.

"You want a drink or a tip?" Castle asked the driver.

"Hair of the dog."

"Well, then, sit down, pour yourself one and zip your lip for awhile, difficult as that might be—no offense—and listen to a story about Wyatt Earp.

"All right then," Laramie said. "Where was I?"

"Newman Clanton was saying to you…" Frontenac said.

"He said to me, 'Laramie you look like a tough young hombre. Now, I'm after revenge, want to get them murdering Earps…'"

Castle opened the envelope under the table and removed two ocean liner tickets to neutral Portugal. The dates of departure were not filled in. There was also money in the envelope. Castle didn't know how much. It was in Francs and Pesos, American dollars and British pounds.

He put the tickets back in the envelope and the envelope back in the jacket. Louise was looking at him across the table. He winked.

"'I got one worthless son left, which is Billy who was wounded outisde the livery stable,' Newman said to me. 'And one good son, name of Phineas but he's only thirteen years old. Now what I have in mind is you rounding up some men and going after them Earps. I hear they lit out for California…'"